VISION QUEST

VISION QUEST

A Novel by *Terry Davis*

The Viking Press   New York

For Roy and Lucille Davis

First published in 1979 by The Viking Press
625 Madison Avenue, New York, N.Y. 10022
Published simultaneously in Canada by
Penguin Books Canada Limited

LIBRARY OF CONGRESS CATALOGING IN PUBLICATION DATA
Davis, Terry.
Vision quest.
I. Title.
PZ4.D2645Vi [PS3554.A9377] 813'.5'4 79–10297
ISBN 0–670–74722–X

Acknowledgment is made to Mrs. E. L. Masters
for permission to quote from "Davis Matlock"
from *Spoon River Anthology*
by Edgar Lee Masters.

Printed in the United States of America
Set in Baskerville

. . . I say live it out like a god
Sure of immortal life, though you are in doubt,
Is the way to live it.
If that doesn't make God proud of you
Then God is nothing but gravitation,
Or sleep is the golden goal.

"Davis Matlock" from
Edgar Lee Masters's
Spoon River Anthology

I

Both Dad and I are pretty sure Shute is going to grind my body into the green surface of our David Thompson High School wrestling mat. We work hard to put that thought out of our minds, though. I don't wrestle Shute until after the first of the year, when the weights come up two pounds and I move down from the 154-pound class—where I'm already lean—to become probably the world's hungriest 147-pounder. I've got two weeks yet. We also put it out of our minds because today is my birthday and Dad had our 1941 DeSoto reupholstered in the original mohair. He presented it to me this morning in celebration of my eighteen years and my upcoming high school graduation. Still, he couldn't forget my impending doom. After he caressed the leather armrests, rubbed up the bristling new fabric, and spun the big old steering wheel with one finger, he noted that Carla will be able to drive me around in style and solid comfort after Shute breaks all my bones. Carla is my girl friend. She lives with us.

Carla loves the DeSoto. Today we eat our lunch in it and she spreads a red and white checkered tablecloth over the back seat so she won't drip yogurt on the mohair. I sit in front, manning our Sony portable cassette recorder, playing the Beatles' collection and the Stones' "Hot Rocks," eating raw carrots and celery and hardboiled eggs, turning to pure protein before her very eyes as she hands me another carrot. I'm down to 150. Carla climbs in front and rubs the dash and window moldings with a waxed cloth Dad brought her from the store.

Dad's in the car business. People in the car business call their places "stores" now. The name has gone through phases. When I was a little kid playing park league baseball Dad would say he was going to the "garage." And then when I was in junior high playing Pop Warner football he'd say he was going to the "lot." But now it's "store."

I see Belle walking our way as I finally open the car door to head for my English class. The wind blows hard and for a second my eyes hurt from the cold. "Hi, folksies!" yells Belle, slipping and nearly falling on the icy sidewalk. Belle, you crack, don't do any dope in our car, I think to myself, nodding at her.

Belle is the gum-freeze queen of David Thompson High and Carla's best friend after me. She's wrecked a good share of the time, especially at school. She's usually holding dope and I would hate to see her nabbed for it with Carla. It seems that most of the administration and teachers and kids take Belle's space travel for the effervescence of school spirit. I suppose it's because she's a cheerleader and beautiful. There's really not much chance of her getting caught around school, but I still worry.

Belle is friendly and funny and a good person. She's never done me wrong. The chance of her getting Carla in trouble is the only thing I don't like about Belle. I sound like a parent. Carla wouldn't like it if she knew I felt this way. There's probably nothing to worry about. Carla is pretty down on chemicals and kind of down on dope in general, and she's afraid Belle is overdoing it. I doubt Carla would allow Belle to do any dope in her presence.

I'm smiling big and thinking about friendship as Carla waves good-bye with her waxed cloth. I'm also being careful not to fall on my ass. If I'm going to have my coccyx broken, I'd rather Shute did it than this transient and impersonal patch of ice.

Coach Ratta passes me in the gym door. "What do you weigh?" he asks.

"Fifty," I reply, stopping for a bit. We always leave out the one hundred.

His eyebrows rise. "Can you beat Kuchera?" he asks, eyebrows coming down. He knows I can. What he doubts is that I can make 147 without losing my strength.

"Yes," I reply, thinking how much I like Kuch and how badly I can munch his body, and wishing we didn't have to wrestle off for the spot, but not wishing too hard because it will only be for this one match.

"We'll see," Coach Ratta says. He's sure I'm losing my strength.

Coach and most of the team and a lot of other people at school were pretty pissed-off at me for deciding to graduate a semester early. I'll miss a couple league matches and the district and state tournaments. But Doug Bowden, our number-two guy at 154, is undefeated in his junior varsity matches and is going to put a lot of varsity guys on their backs once he gets the chance. I thought about this before I made my decision.

Coach isn't mad any more and neither is anybody on the team. Dad figured from the start it was okay as long as I was sure. And Carla thought it was a good idea, especially since I'd be working full time and earning money to help Dad. It worries my mom a little, but that's her nature.

Senior English is a nice class. We read novels and short stories and we write essays and discuss. Gene Tanneran, our teacher, says we must articulate with both pen and tongue, so he grades us on class participation.

Gene continually tries to bring up his two favorite subjects for ridicule, Richard Nixon and Spiro Agnew. I figure the two sonsabitches aren't worth my time. Gene and Thurston Reilly, who is editor of the school paper and wants to be a muckraking columnist, get the biggest kick out of Nixon's "Checkers" speech, in which the big dick swears that the guys who contributed to his slush fund never asked him for any special favors, points out his sweet wife's respectable Republican cloth coat, and vows ardently never to return Checkers, the lovable cocker sent to him by a Texan who must have been a real dog-hater.

Gene shows the film once a month and he and Thurston just howl. I thought it was funny the first time, but now I think it's sad. The way I see it, if people ever saw or heard that speech and were still dumb or evil enough to vote for the bastard, they deserve everything he'll ever do to them.

Gene's also got a record of Agnew's speeches. He figures Agnew should be public enemy number one for making parents hate and fear their own children. Gene loved it when I told him my dad thinks I'm a pretty good guy and Agnew is a flaming asshole.

4

Tanneran wrestled in high school and college. He asks me what I weigh as we walk out of class.

"I'm down to fifty," I say.

"Fat city!" Gene exclaims, savoring the irony. "You're gonna make it!"

II

We hold our wrestle-offs after our regular practice. That's *after* two hours of exercises, running, takedowns, escapes, reversals, counters, pins, and getting-off-your-back drills. And a pin in a wrestle-off doesn't end the match. The guy who pins gets five points and you keep on going. I'm glad we do it this way. It really gets us in shape. Shute's chances of killing me would be even better if we didn't.

I've avoided Kuch all practice. Otto Lafte tied me to the trampoline as usual on wrestle-off days. We bounce around and wrestle on the trampoline and he always manages to get me on my stomach and then he sits on my back. Once he gets me down it's all over. Otto weighs 243. He stretches the leg straps of my jock around my ankles; then he hooks the waistband through the tramp springs. I think it calms him somehow. Wrestle-offs shouldn't bother Otto—he's been David Thompson's number-one heavyweight for two and a half years. Kuch usually participates in the trampoline ritual. Not that

Otto needs the help. It's just something we do. Sometimes Otto and I get Kuch. Sometimes Kuch and I and Balldozer get Otto. Sometimes we pluck the guy's pubic hair. Little Jerry Konigi is plucked almost bald. He weighs 98 pounds. Everybody takes out his frustrations on Jerry.

Coach Ratta untied me. Then as I jumped down from the tramp he caught me in mid-air and drove me to the mat. He does this all the time. I think he got the idea from Peter Sellers's valet, Kato, the guy who's always sneaking up and attacking him in the Pink Panther movies. Coach says he does it to keep us constantly alert when we're on the mat, and especially when we're in a match and one wrestler has just escaped and gotten to his feet. A lot of guys get taken down at that point in a match. If you're the one who's escaped, you have this tendency to relax, because you've just gotten out of a hold and scored yourself a point—and you leave yourself open to getting taken right back to the mat. And if you're the one who's let the other guy escape, you have this tendency to say shit and shake your head and relax for a second—and then the guy takes you down and gets two more points on you. He let me up without saying a word and turned toward the door to the main wrestling room. I untied my sweat pants and had my eyes on my crotch as I adjusted my jock when he knocked me down again. This time he took me right to my back. I was pinned before I could get my hands out of my pants. I guess Coach doesn't want me getting overconfident.

Not only do we hold our wrestle-offs after a full practice, but we wrestle nine minutes instead of the regular six. And even if you pin or get pinned, you still have to go the full nine.

Kuch is ready. He's spoken with the Everywhere Spirit and now he's shouting his war cries. He took a lot of shit

7

about his Indian stuff from crowds last season, especially on the road. People wrote the principal and called him on the phone to complain about Kuch's aboriginal behavior on the mat. Kuch doesn't consult with the Everywhere Spirit in public any more and the only time he uses his war cry is at the whistle when he's on the bottom in the referee's position. But he still does all his Indian stuff when he wrestles off.

Kuch screams and I bounce into my takedown dance. I'm too fast. I take him down with single-leg dives, double-leg dives, sweeps. I counter his dives with a whizzer, slipping my arm under his armpit to the back of his head and levering downward so he either has to let go of my leg or get flipped over on his back. Each time a takedown is scored we're up and going again. Kuch is strong. If he locks me up he can snap my head down to the mat or shuck me off, spinning me sideways, opening me up for a fireman's carry. I dance away and don't lock up with Kuch. We go takedowns for three minutes and I lead 12–0.

Now we go to the referee's position—one guy down on his hands and knees and the other guy kneeling beside him with one arm around his waist, fingers on his belly button, and the other hand gripping his elbow. The top guy's chin is in line with the bottom guy's spine. They both look straight ahead at the referee's hand, which is supposed to move at the same time he blows his whistle to start the round. The down guy has the better chance to score points. He can escape for one point, or reverse and get control of the top guy for two points. The top guy tries to keep control and work for a pin. In a real match, when you escape you work for a takedown, and when you reverse you work for a pin. But in wrestle-offs, when we get an escape or a reversal we go back to the referee's position and start again.

8

Kuch is down first. He's very strong and he's quick. He pops right to his feet, screaming, trying for an escape. But I go to a double-heel trip and haul him back down to the mat. He's too out of breath now to keep up his steady stream of war cries. I counter his sitout. I follow him on his roll. I try to pin him toward the end of the round, but either I'm too tired or he's not tired enough. I can't take him to his back.

Now I get three minutes from down. I throw my best moves from here. I walk out on him—"crawl" out, actually, charging on my hands and knees, like a giant little kid escaping from his playpen; then I explode into a sitout and reverse for two points. I pop to my feet, bellowing like a goosed dromedary, and use a standing switch for two. I lock his arm and roll, escaping for a point. I buck back and hip over, reversing for two. I throw an outside switch and lean back hard for leverage on the arm Kuch is trying to hold me with. I'm levering hard and have almost worked behind him to gain control when he lets me go and pulls his arm away. I fall flat on my back. He's on me in half a breath and I'm pinned. Renewed, he whoops and dances and kicks me in the ass a few times, smiling. We go back to the referee's position and wait for Coach's whistle.

III

C arla picks me up from practice. Whenever she can she drives me downtown, where I work part-time as a room-service boy at the Spokane Hotel. When she's working herself or when she has something to do, I take the bus or just hitch. There're always plenty of people driving downtown.

"Well?" Carla asks.

"I kicked ass," I reply.

"How badly?"

"Twenty-three to five."

"You got pinned again!" Carla knows how to keep score. I get pinned fairly often in practice, but I've never been pinned in a match.

"Fucking rubber-arm." I sigh, shaking my head.

"What can you do?"

"A guy rubber-arms you when you lean back too hard and hesitate on the switch. You're leaning on his arm for leverage, and if you hesitate at all, he can pull his arm away. You fall right on your back. I've got to stop hesitating. Either that or go to a sitout or a standup all the time."

"Is Shute a good rubber-armer?" Carla asks.

I squinch my face.

"I know," she says. "Is a pig's pussy pork?"

I have to laugh. That's one of our local clichés from which Carla usually refrains. She must have been keeping it in reserve for just such an appropriate moment. "Gotcha." She smiles smugly.

We stop at Strick's bakery. Carla likes to buy day-old doughnuts and maple bars for Dad's breakfast. Carla eats granola and Dad has eggs, meat, and a doughnut or a maple bar. I drink a can of Nutrament, and if my weight's down enough I might eat a slice of liver or a wheat-germ burger, too. Having breakfast together like that is a good way to start the day.

"Is the exhibitionist still in the hotel?" Carla asks. Part of the fun of working in a hotel is all the weird people you meet. I try to keep Carla informed about them.

"I guess," I reply. "I'm pretty sure he's a homosexual."

"Why?" Carla asks.

"Because," I say. "He was naked again, toweling off after a shower like he always is. But this time he drops the towel, flashes me a shot at his root, and gets an immediate hard-on. His cock jerked up in stages like a drawbridge. I just stood there. I told him to give me a call when he was through. I meant so I could pick up the tray. He just smiled and scratched his nuts."

"The human body well kept is a beautiful thing," Carla says. "I don't think there should be any limits to the fun people can have with it." Then she says, "And I think your friend Tanneran is after mine."

"Your what?" I ask. I'm a little tired and slow-witted after a hard practice.

"My body," Carla says.

"What makes you think that?"

"He asked me to come to his house."

Gene's my friend, so I have my doubts about the sexual nature of his invitation. Maybe Carla's flattering herself. It could be true, though. Gene's a very horny stud and he's got what they call a "penchant" for high school girls. He's also got good taste and Carla is dynamite subdued. Maybe Gene just doesn't know Carla and I are together now.

"Do you want him?" I ask.

"No."

"Would you like me to talk to him about it, then?"

"Yes," Carla says. "But not because I can't. It would just make me feel better about us. Okay?"

"Sure," I reply. Now I'll have to talk to Tanneran. Shit. But it's good of Carla to let me know what she expects of me. Having a serious girl friend is not all fun and games. There's responsibility in it.

Carla is related to the reason I'm working during wrestling season. It was partially because of Carla that Dad lost his job and is being sued for fifteen thousand smackers. He decided he didn't want to work for anybody else again, so he sold our cabin at Loon Lake and our boat and pickup, borrowed a bunch of money, and opened Spokane's first Honda car store. Shortly after Dad lost his job he and Mom broke up. He lost our poodle in that deal, and I lost part of my mother. I felt like I should help Dad, so I sold my 450cc Honda motorcycle and vowed to work as steady as I could through the school year to earn money for college. This was one of the big reasons I decided to graduate early. Chances are I'll get a wrestling scholarship, but they don't pay for everything. I had other reasons, too.

Carla walked into the store one afternoon last July with three hundred bucks. She'd been hitching since Chicago and was fed up with it and wanted to buy a car that would get her to the Pacific Ocean. The store was a big Buick dealership downtown near the freeway and Dad was sales manager. Dad was out when Carla came looking for a car. Ray Lucas, one of the used-car salesmen, showed Carla the back row, where all car dealers keep their clunks. In the back row last July sat a '62 Rambler wagon, a '65 Imperial, a '49 Chevy pickup, a '66 Buick, and a '53 Ford coupe. I remember because Dad and I were looking for a cheap car to run as a claimer in the stock car races. I was all set to buy that Ford if it was any good at all. I figured to bash out the windows, rip out the upholstery, and weld in a rollbar. I'd dropped by after work that day so we could test-drive it. Dad thought the bearings might be about gone.

I saw the commotion from way down the street. Five or six people were gathered on the sidewalk, looking through the cars toward the back of the lot. I walked the Honda through them, then rolled down the driveway and pulled up next to Ray Lucas. He was leaning against the trunk of a '71 Buick, looking down at the bloody dentures in his hand and the spots of blood that ran down his white shirt and burgundy pants and onto his white shoes. Dad was talking to a girl about my age who instantly reminded me of a Raggedy Ann doll. In one hand she clutched a bouquet of paper money, and from her shoulder hung a cheap packsack out of which poked a beat-up cardboard sign that said west. The old Ford coupe hung from the company wrecker in the alley. The girl stuffed the bills in her packsack, then tore off her shirt and wrapped Dad's bleeding hand in it. She wore a man's white cotton tanktop undershirt, through which her beautiful round breasts were visible to the crowd of

13

us. Dad tried to take off his suit coat to put it around her, but he couldn't get his sleeve past the wad of flannel.

"Your fucking father cracked up," Lucas gummed.

Two bike cops pulled in, flanking me, followed by an ambulance. They leaped off their bikes and grabbed my arms. "Dad!" I yelled. He turned and ran toward us, waving his bloody flannel mitt.

"It's not the kid!" yelled Lucas. "That's the one!" He pointed at Dad. "The guy's gone crazy."

The cop let me go and raised his hand in front of his chest to show Dad to keep his distance. Dad slowed down and walked the rest of the way to where I sat on the bike. "It's all right," he said to the cop. "It's all over." He rested his elbows on my headlight and sighed.

"What happened?" I asked.

"I don't mind a man making money," Dad said. "But I don't like him stealing it."

"What happened?" I asked.

"Your fucking father flipped out is what happened," Lucas said. He shook his bloody dentures in Dad's face. "This crazy bastard broke my teeth!" he yelled at the cops.

The ambulance attendant made Lucas lie down on a stretcher. "For Chrissake," said Lucas. "I'm all right."

"We got a call somebody was hurt," the guy said.

"Well, it ain't me," Lucas replied.

One of the cops took Lucas's statement and the other took Dad's. All of us, except Dad, leered at the girl. "Fuck you guys!" she screeched, giving us the finger. She turned and fingered the mechanics who stood looking at us from the shop door. She fingered the salesmen looking at us from behind the showroom window.

The ambulance attendant taped Dad's hand and the girl grabbed her shirt from my handlebars.

"Pull that Ford in, park the wrecker, and go down to

The Shack and wait for me," Dad said, flipping me the wrecker keys. "Buy her a sandwich," he said, pointing to Carla.

Carla and I walked the six blocks to The Shack. I'd have taken her on the bike if I'd had an extra helmet. But I didn't, so I had to push it along the curb. First a guy in a Dodge van stopped to give me and the bike a lift; then a guy in a Toyota pickup stopped. By the time I told them I was just walking with a friend who didn't have a helmet and thanked them for the offer, Carla was two blocks down the street. I pushed the bike at a dead run to catch her.

"I'm Louden Swain," I puffed. "That guy back at the car lot was my dad."

"I know," she said.

"What's your name?" I asked. God, she was beautiful. She had curly red hair that blew a little in the breeze. Her nose was small and her face was lightly freckled. Her breasts swayed slightly at the speed she walked.

"Carla," she replied.

"What happened back there?" I asked.

"According to your dad, that guy he punched sold me the car for too much money."

"How much did you pay?"

"A hundred and forty dollars."

I could have bought that old Ford for fifty bucks. Lucas sold it to Carla for $140. Dad and I could have dropped another engine in it for that kind of money. She thought she was getting a deal because Lucas filled it with gas. Someone had primered it without sanding, so from a distance the finish looked fuzzy. Carla got off on the idea of a fuzzy car. She also liked all the space created by its lack of a back seat. "Lots of animals could have ridden there," she said. She made it as far as the freeway ramp.

We got to The Shack and Carla went in without waiting for me. I hustled the bike around to the parking lot and was sprinting back to the door when Dad pulled in. I walked over to his car. "That was fast," I said.

"Doesn't take long to lose your job," he replied.

I didn't press for details.

We spotted Carla in a booth at the very back. Dad said hello to all the waitresses and to six or eight guys in coats and ties seated at the counter and in the booths. They acted a little funny, so I figured maybe they'd already heard what had happened. The Shack's right on what they call "auto row," so a lot of car-business guys eat there. I'd been meeting Dad for lunch or dinner at The Shack for as long as I could remember. When I was real young Mom would dress me in little suits with hats and short pants and take me down to show me off. Then when I got older I'd take the bus by myself.

"Sorry about putting you through all that," Dad said to Carla.

"I'm sorry about the trouble I've caused you," she replied. "And thanks very much for getting my money back."

"That's all right," Dad said. "That's all right."

Dad ordered breakfast, which he eats any time of the day or night, and Carla ordered a burger. I drank water and sucked the ice. It was only a couple weeks before this that I'd decided to drop to 147 for my last high school wrestling season. Normally I wouldn't have begun dieting until September to reach my usual 154, but I was trying to be as slow and gentle with my body as I could so that in December, when the time came to coax out those seven extra pounds, I'd have its loyalty. I weighed 176 then.

"You can stay with us if you want," Dad said.

"Sure," I said. "We've got plenty of room."

"We'll find you a decent car," Dad said.

"Sure," I said. "For a hundred and forty bucks we can find you a car that'll get you anywhere you want to go."

"That's very, very kind of you," replied Carla.

Mom told Dad Carla was dirty. Carla's jeans were a little mungy, but she was clean. She washed her panties in the sink in the basement bathroom and hung them from the shower-curtain rod. A little spot of blood shown faintly. I figured she was having her period. She rinsed the sink after she brushed her teeth.

Dad gave Carla my bedroom. I could have slept on the davenport in our other basement room, but Mom wanted me to sleep upstairs. Since she and Dad slept in the two upstairs bedrooms, I would have had to sleep on the davenport in the living room. I didn't feel like doing that, so I moved out to the back yard. I slept in the carport when it rained.

I was working mostly nights, so Mom and Dad and I didn't see each other very often for the rest of the summer. They were usually asleep when I got home and looked in their rooms to tell them goodnight and turn off their TVs. And I was usually asleep when they came to tell me good-bye on their way to work in the morning. Dad would come about 7:30. His footsteps were louder across the cement and he never came all the way to my cot. Sometimes his footsteps would wake me and sometimes it would be his voice from the corner of the garage saying, "So long, Son. Be careful on that goddamn motorcycle." An hour later I'd wake to the tap of Mom's high heels or to her hand messing with my hair and her voice saying, "Bye, Sweetie. Hope you make lots of tips tonight." I regret not seeing Mom more often then, because she left us for a china-and-glassware man at the end of the summer, and I'm afraid it was the last chance I'll have in my life to live with her. I don't think she left because of Dad's losing his job and selling the cabin and getting sued and stuff. After Mom started to get well she really got into her job selling china and glassware at the Bon Marché. There may be such a thing as a china-and-glassware syndrome. She had already begun to fall away from Dad before Carla and the lawsuit.

Even in the best of health Mom is built like a falling leaf. But even when she was the sickest her body couldn't keep her spirit down all the time. She always wanted to know what was going on at school and how many cars Dad sold. She was into painting by numbers and making ceramic ashtrays and mosaics—stuff she could do lying down. And when she felt good enough to get around she cleaned the house and washed clothes and baked stuff and even trimmed the grass. We lived in a time of strange eclipse then—all darkness and quiet for part of the month, then blasts of steady light and activity. I know I'm still shaped by those times, but I don't know quite how.

I guess Mom had a terrible time giving birth to me. I heard she almost died. I know something happened to screw up her menstrual cycle and cause her really unnatural pain and heavy bleeding about ten days each month. I have no idea what this problem could have been. I've never come across symptoms like those in my reading. I'd like to ask a doctor.

Anyway, Mom was sick like that for fifteen fucking years. She didn't have a hysterectomy because her doctor, a Naturopath, told her she wouldn't be a woman any more if she did. He also told her that God was the greatest healer.

He treated her with vibrating machines, hot and cold towels, and a lot of capsulated herbs named just with letters of the alphabet. I don't know what God treated her with.

After school I'd take a bus to the clinic to see her. She'd be strapped in this thing that looked like a chastity belt. It was hooked up to an electronic device that resembled an automatic washer on wheels. Violet tendrils of light popped and danced in the little round window. Mom would spend some time hooked up to that machine, then she'd get a series of hot and cold towels, then she'd swallow two Cs and an A and a B, and I'd push her out in her wheelchair. She hurt so bad she couldn't even stand up. We'd take a cab home.

Mom was a country girl and had gone to that guy all her life. She wasn't and isn't terribly religious, so more than that it was probably habit and faith in an old acquaintance that kept her with him. It just happened that after she married Dad and moved to Spokane this doctor decided to open a big clinic here.

Finally, when I was fifteen, the Naturopath died. Mom didn't know any other doctors, so she went to Dad's. Although he never bought the line himself, Dad kept quiet about Mom's Naturopathy for all those years. He just paid the bills.

Dad's doctor referred Mom to a gynecologist, who told her she was crazy for not getting a hysterectomy fourteen years before. So she got one. And after she rested a while she felt great. I don't know if she felt less a woman.

I remember one thing from the days of her sickness—I'll never forget it. I was playing Pop Warner football then. I was in the seventh or eighth grade. Our season was over and I got voted most valuable player. I was a really big bastard for a seventh or eighth grader, so it wasn't surprising. But it was still a pretty big deal for me. I ran home about a thousand miles an hour to tell Mom and show her my trophy. I blasted in the door and saw all the lights were off. I figured she might be sleeping, so I walked quietly into her bedroom. Outside it was a beautiful fall afternoon, and inside there was my mother with her curtains all drawn up tight, curled up like a little animal in her bed, holding her pelvis and crying.

I burst into tears. I must have scared her. I ran up and jumped on her bed and probably half crushed her. I just hugged her and cried like a little kid. All I said was, "I'm sorry you don't feel good, Mom." I just kept saying that. She probably couldn't hear me anyway through all my blubbering.

After a while I showed her my trophy. Mom said she was feeling better and that she thought the trophy was great. Then I went downstairs and cried by the furnace, where Dad used to beat on me when I was little. I fell on the floor like I was having a fit. I remember the concrete was cold at first but got really warm. If that doctor were alive today I'd kill the cocksucker with my bare hands.

After Mom got feeling good she took a job in the china and glassware department of the Bon Marché. In about six months she became a buyer.

I think maybe what happened is that she had been sick for such a long time that finally feeling good was like becoming a new person. She started making friends at work and really got into her job. That's when she starting falling away from us.

None of us was home much. Dad worked a fourteen-hour day, I was either in school or working out or running room service at the hotel, and Mom was traveling a lot. When we were all home at the same time, Mom was busy with her catalogues. The talking she did do was more to Poodle than to Dad or me. But when I'd stop to see her at the Bon, she'd be blustering around in full bloom, gabbing with the sales people and the customers.

She went for a ride on my motorcycle once. It was dusk. I took her up to Manito Park to see the rose garden. She really enjoyed it. But then I took High Drive home and scared the hell out of her. That was a bad move, because she wouldn't go again. I think she got a kick out of riding slow. She wore this long wild scarf from Italy. It flapped about three feet behind us. Mom looked pretty racy. From a distance she probably looked like my little sister.

I think more than anything else it was the change in their life-styles that broke Mom and Dad up. Before last spring Dad was into one thing only—selling lots of cars and making heavy bread. He went at it like a war. Each car sold was an enemy casualty. If he made his bonus each month it was a battle won. He was the general and the salesmen were his troops. He took care of them like a father, selling cars himself and crediting the deals to the lowest men on the board. He wore his uniform proudly—doubleknit sport coat, cranberry slacks, white belt, white shoes.

Mom liked driving her Buick convertible and buying different-colored carpet for each room in both the house and the cabin and buying new credenzas for all her dishes and going out to dinner a lot. The thing about Mom is that she got real pleasure out of this sort of shit. I saw it in her face when she dusted the furniture or when she set the table for company. That's why I don't think I can ever stay pissed-off about it for long. Her family was poor. I guess she learned to need stuff like that by not having it, the same way rich people learn to need it by having it. I don't really understand about learned behavior patterns yet. We're well enough off. At least we were. I couldn't care less about a bunch of fucking cups and saucers or a whole store full of big-assed cars.

Anyway, it happened that Mom's new life-style and Dad's old life-style coincided, or at least didn't conflict.

But about last spring Dad began to change. He began to tell me how shitty the new cars were, about how there were so many piddly little things always going wrong with them, and about how they would come from the factory with the armrests half off and the plastic "wood" on the dash coming unglued. He complained to the factory representative that nothing manual could be ordered any more—no standard transmissions, brakes, or steering, not even a station wagon back window that could be rolled by hand. The factory man, this young college-educated guy of whom Dad had been in awe, told Dad that people didn't want to do things by hand any more. Dad, who was getting less and less awed all the time, said, "In a pig's ass they don't!"

Then I began seeing books on the nightstand with Dad's *Time: Future Shock, The Assassin Automobile, The Human Use of Human Beings, Power and Innocence.* He began to wear his older, plainer clothes. He's got two closets full of clothes. He must have a hundred shoes. He quit smoking, and to fight his nervousness he built a working model of the Wankel engine. He tried to talk Mom into quitting smoking. He tried to talk her into selling the Buick and buying a little Honda car. He wanted to try walking to work a couple days a week. Mom was having none of it.

One evening after I got home from working overtime I heard Mom and Dad talking. Dad was nearly pleading with her to stop smoking. She smokes about three packs a day. I was surprised at Dad's tone. I'd have to call it "tender." I wouldn't call him mean, but I don't usually call him tender, either. It made me happy in a sad way. Not that it turned out well. Mom said she loved smoking and could never quit. The tone in which she said it made me feel strange and good. I would have to call it tender, too. She also said it would break her heart to sell the convertible. She said she'd never drive "one of those little toilet bowls."

Dad hasn't smoked a cigarette since. But he did return

to cigars, of which he smokes probably fifteen a day.

Either Mom and Dad ended their twenty-year marriage quietly or they did all their yelling when I wasn't around. The first I knew about it was one day in the middle of August when Mom asked me to meet her for lunch. We sat in a booth in the Bon Marché cafeteria and Mom told me she was moving to Seattle.

I focused on the way she held her cigarette. So casual —elbow out, wrist cocked, a little kiss of lipstick on the filter. I thought back to the picture I'd seen of Mom in her teens, when her hair was long in what they called a "page boy." And in my mind I could see her practice holding her cigarette. Stuff like that was important then. I loved my Mom that day as much as I ever did or probably ever will. I think I loved her because she suffered so long and still came out of it with a good heart. Maybe I feel guilty for being part of the cause of her suffering and love her to make up for it. Whyever I love her, I don't think it's just because she's my mother.

"Punkin," Mom said. "I want you to know they broke the mold when they made your father."

So Mom lives in Seattle with her new husband now. She transferred to the Seattle Bon Marché. We talk more now, even though it's only over the phone. I'll spend a week with her after the season's over. The University of Washington invited me to visit their campus, so I'll do that then, too. Carla doesn't think she'll go along.

IV

It's dinner time at the hotel and Elmo, the cook, asks me what it will be. I tell him a wheat-germ burger. Lean beef mixed with wheat germ. He keeps a couple in the fridge for me.

Elmo is a big fan of the semipro football team I played a little for this fall. He thinks I'm crazy to lose all this weight just to get my body thrashed. He wants to see me play college ball, then go to the pros. There's no way. I even got beat up playing my one season of high school ball. I tell him *he's* the crazy one. "Those guys are creatures," I say. "They'd peel me and eat me!"

The Spokes picked me up as a flanker. I'm pretty fast and I catch the ball. I'm not crazy about getting hit, though. They paid me twenty bucks a game. I was making pretty good money working five nights a week at the hotel and playing ball on Sundays. Otto played, too, but much more seriously than I did. Otto is a real football player. Football's what will get him through college, and unless he gets hurt or something, he'll go with the pros for sure.

Tanneran played guard and Leeland Wain, the David Thompson varsity football coach, played quarterback. I'm pretty good friends with both Gene and Leeland, considering our age differences.

I had to go out to Rollie's Ribs after the game to pick up the extra tens this gambler friend of Elmo's gave me for each score. Now that it's legal to drink on Sundays, Rollie's really blasts after the games. One night some other friend of Elmo's was drinking or doping or both and decided I was white-assed and chicken-shit and that he was going to cut me up and feed me to Rollie's Afghan hound. I thought he described me pretty well and wasn't about to argue. When he started after me with the world's biggest pocket knife, all I could do was stand open-mouthed and greasy-handed. Stuff like that scares me even in the movies and it was twice as scary in real life, especially coming so fast out of a situation where everything had been peaceful and fun. Leeland got up to stop the guy and the guy took a swipe at him. Then Elmo got up and the guy took a swipe at him. Then Tanneran picked up one of those round-bottomed wine bottles they use for candle holders and cold-cocked the guy. It wasn't funny. The bottle broke and the guy went down like he was dead. Gene went back to his ribs and Elmo dragged the guy outside. I was grateful to Gene, but since then I've been a little afraid of him. He got so mean so fast, and then he was so normal again. I still like the guy a lot and I admire him, but I'm not too anxious to talk to him about Carla.

Elmo says, "You my mainest man, though you dumb."

The dinner orders have started to come in. Sally, the cashier, hands me the slips. Number 611 is on top. Crab

Newburg, tea, lemon pie. He's still here. I give the slips to Elmo and he hands me my solitary burger.

I have no control—it's gone in two bites. Christ, I'm hungry! I fight it with a book of fiction.

I read quite a bit. This may be why I've done pretty well in school so far. There may be a correlation between reading a lot and appearing to know things. Downstairs in the employees' bathroom, along with my secondhand copy of Gray's *Anatomy*, I've stashed *The Confessions of Nat Turner*. At home in the downstairs bathroom I keep *Pathology*, a gigantic book by a physician named Robbins. When I'm tired of reading it I balance it on my head to strengthen my neck. Upstairs at home I keep Upjohn's *Manual on Nutrition*. I don't use the upstairs bathroom that much, and I'll go with Adelle Davis on the subject of nutrition, at least until I'm something other than a layman in the field.

Next to messing around in the woods up along the Columbia where Dad grew up, I'd have to say that learning about the human body is the thing that interests me most. Next comes the human mind, I guess, or the human heart—whatever it is that makes us act the way we do. I love reading and watching movies and talking with my friends, even standing with a tray of dirty dishes and eavesdropping on the guests at the hotel, gossiping over their dessert. Wrestling combines these things for me.

After I first thought seriously about a profession I decided I'd become an exobiologist. I was going to be one right up until the start of this season. Since I'd decided to try to come down a weight class and give Shute a go, I thought I'd consult a specialist about my chances of losing 29 pounds while still retaining enough strength to shake hands before Shute osterized my body. So I made an appointment with a nutritionist. His office was in a huge old house on the Southside near where Mom's

Naturopath had had his clinic. An old Mercedes 190 SL sat halfway in the garage. I couldn't tell what year it was. If it was the doctor's, he sure had good taste in autos. If the guy did his own decorating, he also had good taste in furnishings. The place was paneled in brown leather, carpeted wall to wall in a dark wine color, and filled with black crushed-leather chairs and davenports. It was also filled with some very svelte ladies and a few hog bodies. I was the only guy. I was surprised when I got to see him —he looked like a regular young doctor. He asked what it was he could do for me. "Consultation," I said. He looked at me as though I'd called him a chiropractor. He said he didn't hand out pills. I told him I didn't take pills, except vitamins. He thought I was after some speed. I told him how much weight I needed to lose, the length of time I had to lose it, and why. I explained that I thought I could do it if I kept to 1000 calories a day and kept my nitrogen balance positive. I described my workout and my diet, relating the luck I'd had in the past with vitamins E and B_{12}. He grimaced when I mentioned Adelle Davis. Before I could ask his opinion he was up and out the door. I sneaked a look at the chart he'd written up on me. After my name it said, "Hippy health nut; hard drug symptoms." I'd put it down and was puzzling over some possible "hard drug symptoms" when he came back with a vial of Gaudium and told me to eat, even if I wasn't hungry. Then he walked into the next examining room, where reclined the sveltest of the svelte. I was so stunned I missed what was surely a terrific shot at her pudenda. Driving home, I regained my composure enough to be pissed-off. I gave the capsules to Otto. He loves that shit. Pops those things like Life Savers and still he eats like a catfish.

I'd figured I would hit it off with a nutritionist, that I'd develop some rapport and go back to him for the two physicals I'd need for the season. You have to get one before the first league match, and then you have to get another one if you plan to drop down a weight when the classes come up.

Dad's doctor is a myopic old fart who laughs like hell at me anytime I use a medical term or ask a medical question. He makes me feel about as intelligent as a grapefruit. But he set Mom straight as an arrow, so I don't mind going to him instead of a nutritionist. I don't know the extent to which he relies on God's healing powers. Lucky for me I went to see him. He had this medical student with him from some place in Ohio, doing what they call a "preceptorship," which is a brief practical introduction to the kind of medicine you intend to practice. You live with the doctor and see what it's really like to be one.

The medical student's name was Max Mokeskey. Max was doing his preceptorship in Spokane so he could hike in the mountains and fish in the lakes and streams and hunt birds in the Palouse. I liked him. He laughed at me and told me I was full of shit and that I'd surely die if I tried to hit 147. I told him I'd already come down from 176 to the 155 I weighed then. That impressed him. We talked for a couple hours. Old Dr. Livengood wanted him to get to know patients. He said that was the essence of a successful family practice. We talked about my plans and his plans and about hiking and fishing and hunting birds. While we talked I got my physical and was informed I had a roving testicle. Max called my exobiology idea bullshit. He said few specialists in any field of medicine have time to do anything but read their journals and be present at the auditing of their taxes. He said family practice gives you at least a little time to yourself and a chance to have relationships with your patients as people instead of just diseases. He also said there are few trout streams out in space, where exobiology will be practiced when I finish med school. He didn't actually convince me, but he sure was a lot better example of a physician than that nutritionist.

I don't know what kind of doctor I want to be. For now I've got to be a teratologist and study that monster Shute.

Whatever kind of doctor I become, I hope I always make time to read and see movies and talk about them with my friends. I hope I meet people in college who like to do this. When I get home tonight I'll proofread a paper I wrote on *The Water-Method Man,* a novel by John Irving, who is a former wrestler. The paper is for a course I'm taking by mail from Eastern Washington State College. I wrote my last one on Don DeLillo's *End Zone.* I got a B. The instructor wrote that my approach was too personal and that I misunderstood the book. He said it was a metaphor, not about football at all. Beats me what it would be a metaphor for. Carla thought it was about how living with the bomb fucks us up. I still think it was about football.

I'm almost a college sophomore in terms of credits. I hope to be one by the time I graduate. They don't let you take pre-med courses by mail, so I'm getting some other basic stuff out of the way. I finished my high school biology, chemistry, physics, and calculus last year. Each morning during my two study halls, if I don't go for a workout, I read Dr. Ralph Besson's *Obstetrics and Gynecology.* So far I only understand the conjunctions. Dr. Besson is down at the University of Oregon, but I didn't get to meet him when I was invited down there. About all I ever get to talk to when I'm invited to a college is the athletes and occasionally a sorority girl.

I feel spacy now, light-headed. My hunger is out of control. I'm a little nervous to read anatomy, so I sit here on the employees' toilet with a good story. I'm just to the part in Styron where Nat is given to the Reverend Eppes, who, as Styron says, "gropes malodorously" after Nat's "virgin bum." I linger over the passage.

Elmo has the order ready. I take it on a cart rather than a tray, thinking I want to have my hands free.

The guy is nude again, I know. I can hear the shower running.

He is. He stands shivering and toweling, his stubby cock flapping. I push the cart past him, in front of the mirror.

In the mirror I see him come up behind me. He's a round man. Young, maybe thirty, but getting bald. He's hairy as hell—like me. He takes care of himself, and that's not easy for an endomorph.

I see myself staring at him. He's smiling. His cock cranks up. He drops the towel at my feet. I'm sweating, and I don't sweat much any more. My hands shake on the edge of the cart. Softly he knocks me into it. The dishes clank. The tea spills a little. The lemon pie quakes. He's shorter than I am, almost resting his head on my shoulder. He brings his hands around and cups my cock. I had a hard-on before I came in. He sighs. I have a pretty big cock. His head rests on my shoulder.

"Would you like me to blow you?" he asks.

I look in the mirror. I look scared and he sees it. But I'm not scared of him. I breathe deep. We sometimes get four thousand people in our gym for a match. I hear them roar, chant for a takedown, a reversal, a pin. I breathe deep and stop shaking. If I ever experiment with this stuff, it won't be now.

"No, thanks," I reply.

He backs off, looking at me in the mirror.

"Don't be nervous," he says. "Would you like to look at some pictures?"

"No, thanks," I say at the door.

I do a hundred pushups before the elevator reaches six.

V

I leave my white shirt and black slacks in my hotel locker, stuff my school clothes into my packsack, and run home in my rubber sweat suit. I look pretty weird running down Riverside. But it's 11:30, so downtown Spokane is pretty deserted. Fridays and Saturdays you can't get across the street for all the kids cruising. I run down alleys on Fridays and Saturdays.

Up on the Northside a two-cycle bike blows by me, wound tight. It must be Kuch!

This is mid-December. The streets sparkle. The moon is cold. Nobody rides in December in Spokane.

Whoever it is brakes and goes down, sliding a half-circle, ramming the snowbank at the curb.

It is Kuch! I know his fall. We haul his bikes to the races in Dad's truck when Kuch's dad has to work. Kuch is good. No shit. He's already an AMA Junior, and I bet he makes Expert next year. He's mainly a motocross rider. He spends all his money on his racers. He's got two 360 Yamahas—one for motocross and one for flat track and TT. I don't know what Kuch would do if he had a choice between living his life over as an Indian in the early 1800s or becoming a world-class motocross rider.

"I came down to the hotel to see you," he says, looking up at me.

"You okay?" I ask.

"Sure," he says. "You kicked the holy living shit out of me today," he says, getting up.

"I'm bigger than you are," I say.

"You'll murder Shute," says Kuch. "You'll pound up on him."

Kuch knows plenty about Gary Shute. Shute's been the only guy to pin him in the past two years. Shute pinned him six times. Twice in duel meets, twice at district, and twice in the state tournament. In this case, however, Kuch's perspective may be clouded. He's my friend.

"Tell my dad," I say. "He's already taking contributions for the Louden Swain memorial fund."

"You and your dad are both nuts," Kuch says.

Kuch rides slow while I run. "How many miles you do a day?" he asks.

"Three," I reply. "Not enough."

"Were you really trying to pin me in the second round?"

"Busting my ass. Do you realize how tough that sonofabitch Shute has become since last year?" I rave. "He carried his dad's console TV up and down the stadium steps a hundred times—running! Then his dad had to use a live wire on him to keep him from eating it. He'll kill me and drag my body around school behind his fucking Camaro. He'll ravage Carla. He'll throw our guppies off the water tower. Three miles ain't enough."

"I hate the fucking *Iliad*," Kuch says. Beyond motorcycles and American Indians, Kuch's interests are pretty limited.

"He's worried about you," Kuch says when we hit the park. "Laurie works with his girl friend's cousin. She says Shute's given up fucking."

"The guy has no soul," I puff. "I'm glad I didn't play school football this year. He would have collapsed my lungs, ruptured my spleen, wailed on my mailbox." Shute is a high school all-American in football and wrestling.

"Oh, bullshit," my friend says.

"You got time to do a couple miles with me?" I ask as we hit the track.

"Sure," Kuch says, speeding up.

After the first mile I realize I'm carrying the packsack. I fling it somewhere.

Kuch is riding beside me. "You sure that wasn't a portable TV?" he asks.

"Console," I spit. I'm beat. I begin to lengthen my strides. I suck the air in, count, then blow it out. I puff like an old steam barge. I go loose of mind and body and marvel at the clouds of vapor I emit. Through the pines there must be stars up there somewhere. I think of Dad's stories about before Grand Coulee Dam, about when the Columbia was still a river, and about how the Colvilles camped at Kettle Falls and speared and netted the salmon and dried them close enough to where Dad lived that he could hear the flies buzzing around them as they dried. I see an old steam barge I've only seen in books go steaming up the Spokane, log booms flowing behind like the tail of a peacock. I see Puget Sound. Seattle long before the Space Needle. The lumber schooners docked at Port Blakely, once the biggest mill in the world. I see Shute steaming up the stadium steps with a console TV on his back.

"Don't lay down," Kuch whispers. Snowflakes fall in

wonderful cold explosions on my closed eyes. "Christ, you'll catch cold."

I grab the packsack he hands me. It's like lifting the DeSoto. My head stops strobing by the time we reach our side of the park. I look back at David Thompson Park, thinking most of my life has revolved around this grass, these ball fields, pools, courts, slides, swings, schools. Kuch walks his bike.

"I'll run with you," he says. "You do your three miles in the morning and we'll do two more after practice."

"Gotta be to work by five-thirty," I say.

"I forgot," he says. "After work then. I'll catch you on the way home."

"Right on!" I shout. "You my mainest man!"

VI

D ad is asleep, with his little Sony portable still show-
ing sports news. I turn it off. I turn off his light.
"Night, Son," Dad wheezes.
"Night, Dad," I whisper.

Carla is listening to her Johann Pachelbel record and
studying for her child development test. She takes that
and senior English and contemporary world problems at
David Thompson. All she needs for her diploma is the
English.
I strip off my sweat shirt and throw it into the laundry
room. It sticks to the wall. I do sweat still, if I work hard
enough. I pull off my boots and step onto the scales—
147. Jesus! I walk in to tell Carla, but she grabs me before
I can speak. I smell incredibly bad, but we waltz through
her favorite band on the Pachelbel. It fractures me that
this music is almost three hundred years old.
"What do you weigh?" she asks.
"Forty-seven," I reply proudly.

"Wow!" Carla smiles. "Want me to fix you a treat?"

"Let's have yogurt and pineapple for breakfast," I suggest.

I feel her lips on my abdomen. I curse the remaining adipose tissue lurking in the subcutaneous layers. There can't be much. I flex the muscles of my rectus abdominis. "Narcissus," Carla whispers.

I'm dreaming, but I'm not asleep. Contrary to popular belief, if you're in really great shape you don't need much sleep. I'm so hyper in mind and body, so psyched, I don't feel like sleeping. I lie here and think about Shute, about Mom and Dad, about Carla, and about the short time I've got left to be a kid. And finally I drift into a reverie about the river, about the first time I saw it.

I'm just a little kid—a fat little Cub Scout—and Mom and Dad and I are driving north on 395 toward Colville. Dad was selling Fords then and we're in a Thunderbird. Mom's got her heating pad plugged into the cigarette lighter. She says she's really feeling pretty good and that she's glad she decided to come to the picnic. I'm in back with my face in the blast from the air conditioner.

A new turbine is being put in Grand Coulee Dam, so they've had to let a lot of water out of Lake Roosevelt. The water is so low that my great-grandfather's old homestead and a lot of other people's old homesteads are uncovered for the first time since 1941, when the Columbia was dammed and renamed. There's going to be a big picnic and fireworks. I'm kind of excited to get to see the place where my dad was a kid, but shooting my .22 and eating a lot of great pie and cake and ice cream and seeing the fireworks are what I'm really looking forward to.

We pass through Colville and the little town of New

Kettle Falls and turn onto a dirt road that goes down to the river. It's hot and dry as hell. Dust rolls thick from two pickups ahead of us, and Mom comments on her thankfulness for the air conditioner. We stop on the hillside before going down to the river. It's a beautiful view.

But this landscape is totally new to me and I'm blown away by what I see. Lake Roosevelt has always been at least a half-mile wide here. But now that it's gone back to being the Columbia River it's about a block wide. A little shit like me could fling a rock across it.

"There's Kettle Falls," Dad says to me, pointing south toward the bridge.

I turn and see where the river drops over a cliff onto a rocky bed. Most of the water falls onto a big boulder that looks like a bowl.

"See that big rock that looks like a kettle?" Dad asks, pointing to the rock that's catching all the water. "That's why the Indians called it Kettle Falls. They used to stand on those big rocks there to the side and spear and net salmon."

I am one astonished little kid. I'd been over the bridge and looked down at that exact spot probably fifty times, but none of this had ever been there. At least I couldn't see it.

All the Swains except Grandpa Harry are sitting around my great-uncle Walker's old Chevy pickup. My great-aunt Lola is there with a giant lunch. She says she's saving it until after we take a walk up-river to see the old place. She's waiting for Grandpa Harry to show up. She calls him "brother." She gives me a chicken leg because I'm a kid. My four cousins are a lot older. The two girls are in their teens, and they put lunch on the picnic table. The two guys are out of school and logging. They sit on the fenders of the pickup and drink beer. My dad didn't get married until he was pretty old. He's the oldest of his generation and I'm the only kid left in mine.

Aunt Lola says to Dad that Grandpa Harry has been drinking again. She says she's worried about him. My uncle Bert says Grandpa's been boozing hard. He calls him "Dad." My dad says he'll drive up to Grandpa's cabin if he doesn't show up soon. I hear this clearly from my seat on the bumper of the pickup in the circle of people.

After a while Dad says we might as well walk up to look at the old place. He puts his hand on my shoulder. Mom says she'd better not walk, and the other folks want to wait till the cool of the evening. So my great-aunt, my uncle, and Dad and I walk along the river in the wet sand.

Around a bend, where Lake Roosevelt is normally over a mile wide, the river bends away from us and flows in a narrow channel, leaving a broad mudflat black and shiny as coal. It must have been great farmland. An old jeep is mired up to its fenders in the mud.

"That's Dad's jeep," Uncle Bert says.

We all walk out to where the mud gets over our shoes. I see the stone foundations of buildings, fence posts dripping rusty barbed wire, a rusted-through water trough sticking out of the mud. My grandfather is walking through where one of the buildings used to be. He's talking, but I can't make out what he's saying.

Dad and Uncle Bert walk out through the mud. Lola points out the foundation of the house where she and Grandpa Harry were born. She says my dad and both my uncles and my aunt were born there too. She shows me where the barn was and the baking kitchen and the outhouse. Dad and Bert and Grandpa are standing where the cemetery was. It had three graves, Lola says: my other uncle, whose .22 is mine and kept for me by Grandpa Harry, and my great-grandmother and great-grandfather. They were moved to the New Kettle Falls cemetery before the water rose.

Dad and Uncle Bert come back and tell her that Grandpa is all right. They stay with me while she walks out through the mud. They act strange. Dad turns me around and points up on the forested hill to a bare spot where they used to go sledding in winter. Uncle Bert points way up near the top of the mountain to where his dead brother, Bobby, shot his first deer.

I turn and see my great-aunt holding my grandfather and patting his head like he's a little kid. Soft-hued in their cotton and flannel, fat good old people, they stand in my memory, clinging and shaking, sinking imperceptibly into the mud of Lake Roosevelt.

Sometimes this experience comes back to me in reverie and sometimes it comes back as a real dream. It's changed a lot since the night of the picnic when I first dreamed it and when it got stuck maybe forever in my memory. I guess it's become what I need it to be rather than what it really was. I don't even remember exactly how the day went any more.

I do remember that Grandpa Harry was very quiet when he came to eat with us after they winched his jeep out of the mud, and that in the evening he took me across the river and up on the mountain to his cabin to shoot the .22, and that we watched the fireworks from his porch until Dad and Mom came to take me home.

Grandpa Harry's in a lot better spirits these days. He had just retired from logging then and I guess he couldn't handle that change in his life. The guy gets better as he gets older. And the less he drinks.

Even though it's a sad memory and has the power to depress me bad sometimes, I still like remembering it. It's the only look I've ever gotten into my family history. Beyond my great-grandparents on Dad's side who came to the Columbia from Oklahoma Territory, I don't know anything about my family. I ask, but nobody seems to know where anybody came from. I'm looking into the darkness and feeling Carla incredibly warm beside me. It's very quiet. I think about that day on the river and wonder what was really said and thought out there in the middle of all that mud.

It's 5:30 and time to "rise and shine," as Dad says when he can get up before I do. I feel good and ready to get moving. There's plenty to do. I've got to hide in the shrubs and scare Damon Thuringer's little brother, who delivers our paper, and I've got to run my three miles.

VII

"We may have a guest for breakfast one of these mornings," Dad forewarns us from the door on his way to work.

"Hmmmm?" I look over at Carla.

"Hmmmm?" She looks back.

For the past few weeks Dad has been staying out pretty late on his nights off. Except Monday. On Mondays we watch pro football on TV.

We woke up to lots of snow. I couldn't scare little Thuringer this morning. I knew he'd see my tracks wherever I hid. We sit at the kitchen table and I mention to Carla that we'd better wax the DeSoto tonight. They'll be salting the roads.

"What do you mean 'we'?" she asks. "Have you got an oozling in your pocket?"

An oozling? I think to myself. What the hell's an oozling? Carla is forever making up animals. The oozling is a new one.

"Okay," I say indignantly. "I'll wax it myself."

"I'll wax the DeSoto," Carla says. "I was teasing. You've got to *work*, you've got to *run*, you've got to *study*, and you've got to *sleep*. I'll wax the DeSoto," she says. "And you've got to make love to me. You said it burns up two hundred calories."

"It's the truth," I say.

"How do you like my new animal?" She beams.

"Fine," I reply. "An oozling sounds like a nice animal."

Before we leave I fetch the space heater from the upstairs closet and carry it out to the garage so Carla won't have to look for it tonight.

On the way to school I promise we'll take a picnic out to Seven Mile to see the deer.

Carla didn't take to me right away. She did, however, take to Austin Tower, a Spokane Community College basketball player from New York.

She got a job right off at the New Pioneer, a health food store downtown. That's how she met Belle, who was her first Spokane girl friend. They soon arranged things so they could work the same hours.

Although I prefer the night shift so I can prowl around after work, sometimes in summer I get stuck on days. Some days I'd look out a Main Avenue window after I'd delivered somebody's lunch and see Carla's blue hat with the white polka dots bouncing down the street, her long rusty hair frizzing in curls beneath it like a bizarre noontime sunset.

In late July a higher hat joined her. It was brown leather and floppy-brimmed and belonged to Austin Tower.

Carla and I talked very little last summer. I think she

took me for an archgoon. God knows I have my goonish aspects. I'm not what any truly discerning female would consider good-looking either. I wear my hair pretty short now, so I'm in trouble in the plumage department. I tried growing it long for two years. It grew straight out on the sides and curly on top. My head looked like a floral model of a geodesic dome. My junior year in physics the kids called me "Bucky Head." I retain my pissy-assed little mustache. A guy as generally hairy as I am should be able to grow hair on his upper lip, but I can't. I covet Kuch's hair—ponytailed or braided.

Anyway, Carla and I didn't talk very much back then. She was not impressed with my trophies when I took her down to the basement to show her where she'd be staying.

For a while I thought she had tried to gross me out. She took off her clothes, turned on the shower, and started in. She had a nice body, but she seemed awfully top-heavy and she had stretch marks low on her stomach. Otto has them on his back and shoulders. Then she turned from the shower and sat down on the toilet and peed. I stood open-mouthed. I do that a lot. I'm a pretty fun person to surprise. When she reached for the toilet paper, I split for the other room. All the time she acted like I wasn't even there.

She was unobtrusive through Mom's leaving. I think she spent those three days and nights at the New Pioneer.

I finally decided she really probably hadn't tried to gross me out. I don't think she ever did anything to purposely offend anyone, including me. She worked like crazy keeping the basement clean; she split the dishwashing with me and cooked when Mom went out of town. She even bought food after she got her job. After her first words down at Dad's old store—"Fuck you guys!"

—Carla turned out to be pretty gracious. I felt a real gentleness all around her.

Carla had one record and two prints with her when she came. She played the record low and often. It's a classical record by Johann Pachelbel. Her favorite band on it is "Canon in D Major." It's a simple tune played by three violins and a continuo, whatever in hell that is. The prints are by a French painter named Henri Rousseau and are very colorful and have monkey faces peeking through a jungle inhabited by soft, naked women and creatures I'm not able to identify. Maybe they're oozlings.

Several times Carla told Dad she'd worn out her welcome and each time Dad told her she hadn't. He even lent her the money for a minor operation she had to have. It was a hemorrhoid operation, which I thought was pretty strange for a young girl. But since then I've read that people of any age can have hemorrhoids.

After reading in *Pathology* about some different types of hemorrhoids and "striae," which are stretch marks, I began to wonder if maybe Carla hadn't been pregnant. So then I read about the effects of pregnancy in *Obstetrics and Gynecology* and was pretty sure she had.

It seems that carrying a baby can stretch a woman's muscles so far they can lose their tonicity. That's one of the causes of stretch marks. And in a way it seems to be the same with the veins in the anal canal that become hemorrhoids. When a mother is giving birth there's so much blood being pumped around and so much pressure being exerted that the veins get stretched so far they can't regain their shape. The tissue bursts through the mucous membrane lining the anal canal and hangs around being a hemorrhoid.

I figured if Carla could pee in front of me, I could ask her if she'd been pregnant. So I did.

"Did Dad tell you?" she asked.

"No," I said. "I just thought from your stretch marks that maybe you had been."

"I was," Carla said.

I didn't know what to say then.

"My baby died," she said. "I don't believe in God, but I think it was a blessing."

"That's good," I said, with incredible thoughtlessness. "I mean, I'm sorry it had to be a good thing." Then I shut up fast.

"My milk's almost gone," Carla said. "I had to milk myself for a while."

"Milk yourself?" I'd never heard of that. "I thought women took shots for that. It's supposed to hurt like hell when the milk isn't nursed out."

"It's a wonderful pain," Carla said. "Look."

Carla unbuttoned her shirt and squeezed a breast pretty hard. A bead of milk appeared on her nipple. I felt strange. I'd never seen anything like that before. I thought it was beautiful and sad. She was so beautiful.

"Your breasts have gotten smaller since you came," I said.

"Um-hum," she replied, buttoning her shirt.

That was about all we said to each other for a long time. The intimacy of the talk didn't bring us together or anything.

I didn't learn about Austin Tower from Carla. I first saw him at the YMCA. He'd be there in the evenings playing ball and lifting weights. I hated him right off. He was this really handsome guy, about six-three and maybe 200 pounds. He was the color of a horse chestnut and wore a middle-sized Afro. And aside from being better-looking, he leg-pressed more than I did. Otto barely out-leg-pressed Tower. I don't train with weights, so I really didn't hate him as much as if he'd done more

46

pushups than I, or more dips. I was jealous of Tower's good looks. Not many guys are better-looking than I am from the neck down, but sometimes I think I'd trade all my muscle tone for a better-looking face. I mean I'm not ugly or anything—except maybe for my cauliflower ears. It's just that I've always kind of wished I was good-looking.

Tower and his pals made me look silly on the basketball court. But they could tell by my rubber sweat suit and my hooded sweat shirt and my high-topped wrestling shoes that basketball wasn't my sport. They tolerated me in the pickup games.

"I dig you dudes another day," Tower would say to us in the mirror, tilting his leather hat. The word at the Y was that the University of Washington recruited him out of a New York City high school, then sent him to Spokane Community to get his grades up.

Sometimes I'd see him out at Rollie's Ribs when I'd stop there to pick up a ten-dollar bill or two after a game. Minors aren't supposed to be in there, but the cops must not watch the place very carefully. I think the cops generally try to stay pretty unobtrusive in that part of town. Also, I'm pretty old-looking for my age. I'm the one who buys everybody's beer. Now that I'm eighteen I can do it legally.

The first time I saw Tower out at Rollie's, Carla was with him. They were sitting with Elmo and some guys who played for the Spokes. Elmo saw me and flashed me the big fist, which in Rollie's I returned somewhat self-consciously. Elmo was about to introduce me to Carla when Tower said, "They know each other, man. She lives in his daddy's house."

"Did Dad get to see the game?" Carla asked.

"He had to work," I replied.

I got a bucket of ribs for Kuch and me and split, waving

to everybody. I'd dropped to 168 by then, but dieting in summer was turning out to be way too tough. I rolled the DeSoto toward the Northside with the good night smells coming in the window and the good rib smells coming from the seat beside me and told myself it was best not to overtrain.

Later, as I sat in the park with the bucket of ribs between my legs and a twelve-pack of Coors beer at my side, Kuch came screaming through the trees on his racer, sliding about thirty yards across the grass into the little cove of benches I'd built so the cops wouldn't spot us drinking. The park was deserted. Kids are always making forts out of the benches, so our little hideout aroused no suspicion.

"You crazy bastard," I said. "You get caught riding that thing on the street, they'll impound it. And you can't get to be an AMA Expert with your bike in the police garage."

"No cop car could catch me," Kuch replied, jamming the heel of his hand down hard on a bottle top, popping the cap against the edge of a bench. "I can climb trees on this machine," he said through the foam. "I wouldn't have to outrun 'em. I'd just wick it up a tree and hide."

I told Kuch about my first sighting of Carla's nipples. I said the time she took off her shirt to wrap Dad's hand gave me my only shot. I didn't tell him about how she walked around naked and just peed right in front of me and stuff. I didn't want him to get the wrong impression.

Kuch described how his girl friend Laurie handled his Hodaka in dirt and pointed out the cleanness of the welds on his Yamaha, the new spoked alloy wheels and the new rear disc brake he and his dad had put on that afternoon. He traced a dirt track in the air for me and drew in the ruts and showed me the line he'd ride to stomp ass the next weekend in the race at Post Falls. We wiped our greasy fingers on the grass and stared up at the stars.

We lay back against the Thompson Park benches and talked about how fast our first two years of high school had gone and about how weird it felt to be beginning the last one in less than a month. I was already getting nostalgic thinking about all the great times being over so soon. And it's a lot worse now that I'll be graduating in a few weeks.

Tanneran once told us that college is where you make your lifetime friends. He said college is where you begin your intellectual growing and that you just grow away from your high school friends. I hope that doesn't turn out to be true. I never want to lose the friendship of Kuch or Otto. I guess it can't turn out to be true if I don't let it.

"Ya know what I'm gonna do instead of goin' to college?" Kuch asked, popping another beer.

"Win the Spanish Grand Prix?" I replied.

"Besides that."

"What, then?"

"I'm gonna go on a vision quest," he said.

I didn't say anything for a minute or two. I'd read about vision quests in several books, but I learned the real detailed stuff about them from a book called *Seven Arrows* by a Northern Cheyenne named Hyemeyohsts Storm. The circumstances under which I read that book consisted of Kuch yelling and screaming, "Read this sonofabitching book, man. It is un-fucking-believable!" It has nice pictures, but outside of the part where the Indian kid fucks his mother, I didn't bend the edges of too many pages.

I originally turned Kuch on to the subject of the American Indian early in our sophomore year. I got into it by way of Thomas Berger's *Little Big Man*. From Berger

I went to *Bury My Heart at Wounded Knee,* to *Black Elk Speaks,* and then to everything I could get my hands on. I liked learning about the Indians, but Kuch freaked out. He rampaged through Indian fiction, history, anthropology, and also through the Wickiup Tavern in Springdale on the border of the Spokane Indian Reservation. For a while it looked like I'd created a monster.

"Why a vision quest?" I asked.

"I'd like to see if I can't find my place in the circle," Kuch replied. "I'd like to know why things happen. I wanna get clean." He sat for a while looking down into his beer bottle and then he went on. "That stuff I was into last year was such bullshit. If there really is an Everywhere Spirit, he oughta be plenty pissed-off at me for that."

Kuch was talking about the way he'd acted last wrestling season and on into the spring. He'd wear nothing to school but a pair of deerskin pants and vest and some coyote teeth on a leather thong—in the dead of winter! He'd sit cross-legged on the floor and eat lunch with his hands. And he'd dance and sing and warcry before, during, and after all his matches. I never figured he was being pretentious exactly, because he was sincere. And he really did look like a noble savage. He was heavily tanned from going half-naked all the time and he was in incredible shape from fasting and working out for wrestling. He glowed with suntan and belief and his braided hair hung down to his ass. He was just overzealous, and looking back, I guess he didn't have his beliefs too well in hand.

I feel able to comment on pretension because I pulled some similar shit when I was going through my "I'm-going-to-be-a-doctor" phase. I wrote a monograph on the clitoris and submitted it to the school paper. Thurston Reilly, the editor, figured it for a public service feature and printed it right away. Thurston was expelled from school just seconds after the papers hit the halls, and I joined him a few seconds later. That was the point at which *The David Thompson Explorer* lost its editorial freedom. Kuch was out of school at the time, too. He had refused a directive from the vice-principal to wear more clothes. He was threatening to attack the vice-principal's house, rape his wife, and cut his nuts off and use the scrotum for a medicine bag. They let us back in before Kuch had finished his research on tanning human hide.

Kuch talked on slowly. I popped another beer. "I'm gonna try to use this whole next season like the Plains Indians used their sweat lodge," he said. "And when the season's over, I'm gonna keep a decent diet and try to keep a straight head through the spring races. And when summer comes, I oughta be ready to go somewhere quiet and sit and learn something."

"Who'll you get to talk about the vision with?" I asked.

"I'll get you, if you're still around. But it doesn't matter, really. There's no sense in tryin' to do it right. Hell, I'm no fuckin' Indian. There probably aren't even any Indians left who could do it right. Where'd they go to find a shield maker or a medicine man?" He popped a final beer and rummaged among the bones for a meaty rib.

"Why wait till next summer?"

"That's just the thing," Kuch replied. "I wanna wait. It's gotta stay important for a long time. Indian kids waited a long time. If it's just a fucking Jesus trip, I don't wanna insult the memory of the American Indian by being part of it."

I thought Kuch's idea was a good one then, cheap drunk that I am. But I think it's a good idea now, too. And he's really doing it. He never talks about it, but he's gotten very reserved and a little mystical, so I assume he's going strong. He's very low in his weight class, so I imagine he's fasting most of the time. That's one reason I cleaned up on him so bad. I don't know exactly how Kuch plans to work his vision quest. Indian kids would get the advice of some older guy about what to do. The older guy, who had been on his vision quest already, would tell the kid to go to a hill outside the camp, or if there were no hill, to someplace far away. There the kid would fast and talk to the Everywhere Spirit until he saw a vision or until the Everywhere Spirit talked back. Then he'd return to camp and discuss what he'd felt and seen. I don't think the word "vision" meant strictly that you saw something. Although you might talk with a coyote or ride over the earth on a white buffalo, you might not "see" anything. I take the word more in a philosophical way. Like the way you see yourself in the world. That's the idea of it all: to discover who you are and who your people are and how you fit into the circle of birth and growth and death and rebirth. I can see how you could get pretty far inside yourself sitting naked and hungry and alone on some mountain for a couple days and nights. Storm, in that book *Seven Arrows*, says an Indian kid would come back from his vision quest and explain what he saw to his advisor; then the advisor would interpret the visions and tell the kid how they revealed his true character and the way the course of his life should run. One of the reasons Kuch might be waiting is to give himself time to acquire the wisdom to interpret for himself. That's probably an okay idea. Indian men would go on a vision quest when their medicine was going sour and they needed to change their lives. After they had gotten wisdom from their first vision quest they could interpret later ones for themselves.

Kuch is pretty smart about using wrestling season like a sweat lodge. You're eating pretty well—which is to say damn little and every bit of it real food—and you're in pretty fair shape. The wrestling room is always like a sauna bath and if you get in a good practice you can feel really cleaned out. Sometimes you can even see visions if you get beat around enough.

It was a mellow talk we had that night. I sat and thought what it would have been like to live a hundred years or so ago. I wondered if it was more fun to die of smallpox or cholera than emphysema or cancer of the colon. I looked up at the pines and through them at the stars, some of which probably burned out when my dad was a kid and when his dad was. The Columbia was a river then and Kettle Falls was actually a falls and not just the name of a little town. And I thought that in a few months the greatest time of my life would be over and I'd have to go somewhere and become more responsible and make a new time the greatest of my life.

Kuch wiped the front wheel of his racer with a greasy napkin. "I found out about my headaches," he said. He'd been having awful headaches since racing started in the spring. "It's my braid," he said.

"Your braid?" Kuch's braid still falls ass-length.

"Yah," he said. "I went to a doctor after the Wilbur race. He takes one look at me and grabs hold of my braid. 'You put your helmet on over this?' he asks. 'Sure,' I says. 'There's your problem,' he says. You wouldn't believe how much better my helmet fits with my hair unbraided."

Kuch drove me home through the park so fast the wind pulled tears from my eyes. There wasn't much room on that little racing seat, so I slapped a tight waist on him and hung on for all I was worth. It was so late the eastern horizon had begun to gray and the birds had started singing. I was fast becoming sick.

Carla found me retching in the basement laundry tub.

"Are you okay?" she asked.

"Baarrrrrrrrrff!" I replied.

"Are you okay?" she asked again, a little more concerned.

"Fine, thanks. And yourself?" I gummed, having taken out my partial plate. I'd broken a plate once before by throwing it up in the laundry tub.

"I'm fine," Carla said. "You look like a folding bear hanging over the washtub that way. You're going to hurt your tummels-tummels."

The folding bear was the first of her animals to whom I was introduced.

"My tummels-tummels already hurts," I said, running the water. "What's a folding bear?"

"A bear that folds over things, especially when he's happy," Carla explained.

"I'm not happy."

"I could tell right away you weren't really a folding bear," she tittered. She was a little drunk herself. "You have a very muscular boom-boom," she continued, pulling off my pants.

I hung parallel to the floor, perpendicular to the tub edge, balanced on my "tummels-tummels," my head wedged under the faucet, my legs waving my pants goodbye.

"How did you get so muscular?" Carla asked, toweling me off.

"God's will," I replied.

"You're not one of them, are you?" she inquired, leading me to the davenport. "I refuse to help a drunken Jesus freak."

"Jest," I replied, "frivolity"—bucking up against the pain. "It was probably Him got me into this. He finds ways to get even, even if He doesn't exist."

Carla began to walk on things. I thought I was dreaming. She got up on the other davenport and walked along the top, spreading her arms wide to balance herself. She walked atop the old oak table, then the bar. Her blue hat flopped. Her breasts, which had become amazingly smaller, bobbed in her tanktop. After turning off the lights, she walked along above me, singing a little song called "The Teddy Bears' Picnic." I yearned for a peek at her pussy. I squinted through the night-lite dark. It's not true that seeing a girl naked a few times makes you lose interest in her body.

"Let's be friends," I offered before losing consciousness.

"You hardly ever talk to me," Carla replied. "What do you expect? I thought you were just a dumb jock. I couldn't understand how you could have such a nice father."

"I am just a dumb jock," I said. "But I have a nice father. I'm a little shy," I explained more seriously. "You never talk to me either."

We had nearly formulated a friendship pact when I changed the subject to Grand Coulee Dam and lost consciousness in the middle of invective.

Carla avoided me for a couple weeks after that. She was convinced I was just a dumb jock.

VIII

I n a way it was the Columbia that finally got Carla and me together, and in a way it was Dad. Dad read in the New Kettle Falls newspaper that Lake Roosevelt was being lowered because of some work on the dam, and he told Carla and me that if we drove up there we might get to see the river and the falls. Carla was fired up to go, even if it was with me. I traded my days off to match hers and we were set.

Carla wanted to get an early start. I heard the basement door open and close and then footsteps across the patio. I opened one eye for a second and saw Carla's boots at the edge of my cot. It was still dark. She nudged my shoulder through the sleeping bag. "Louden," she said. "Louden. Time to get up." Her voice was soft. I kept my eyes closed and thought of waking up beside her. "Louden."

"Good morning," I said, opening my eyes. "Thanks for waking me."

"You're sure you're awake?"

"I'm awake. I'll be in in just a sec." Carla went back in and I sat up and rubbed my eyes and peered at my watch. I had to cup my hand around it to read the dim luminous dial. It was 4:30. I checked around to see if she was looking out the door, then jumped up, grabbed my jeans, and ran to the grass behind the house. I had my shorts on, but I didn't want her to see me. My cock stuck out straight as a tent pole.

We still had our '51 Ford half-ton pickup then, so we set the tent and sleeping bags and mason jars that we had to take back to Aunt Lola and ax and shovel and tarp and first-aid kit in the back, since it wasn't going to rain.

It was an incredibly beautiful morning, which is the way most summer mornings are around Spokane. There wasn't a sound and the only smell was freshness. The street lights were still on and the sky was graying into blue. I was stretching and yawning and growling and about fixing to give the neighborhood my Mountain Man good-morning yell when eleven-year-old Dwight Thuringer came whistling down the sidewalk with his newspapers. My hiding was totally unpremeditated. I just whipped into the big shrubs before he saw me. I didn't decide to scare him until he got right to the porch and banged his paper off the screen door. I leaped out and threw my arms in the air and bellowed like a Sasquatch. Little Thuringer screamed and fell back on the lawn in a storm of neatly·folded newspapers. He twitched a little and gurgled in his throat. I was rolling on the lawn, laughing out of control.

Dwight was throwing papers at me as hard as he could when Carla came out. I was still laughing, rolling around, but I was trying to cover up my tender spots. Those square-folded papers hurt. When he got me right at the base of the skull, it sobered me up and I got to my feet and ran around behind the house. I heard Carla ask

57

Dwight what happened. "Goddamn Louden jumped out and scared me," he said. He sounded like he was ready to cry.

I had climbed over the fence and come through the breezeway and out onto the lawn again. "God, I'm sorry, Dwight," I said. "I just couldn't help myself." And then I started to laugh again. But then I saw he had peed his pants and it made me feel ashamed.

Finally Dwight started to laugh, too. He began to pick up his papers and I helped him. "You really scared me," he said. "I must have looked funny."

"You flew through the air," I said, starting to guffaw again.

Carla and I lifted his double bag over his head and brushed the dewy grass off him, ignoring the pee smell, and waved him good morning. I brushed the wet grass off my front and turned for Carla to brush my back. "You're really a bastard," she said, refusing to brush me. I asked her if she wanted to drive and she said she did.

The old Ford had to be double-clutched, and Carla took a while to get the hang of shifting. But once we got out on 395 she didn't have to shift, so the ride was smoother. The windows wouldn't roll up and the heater had a leak, so we were cold till the sun got up a little. I would laugh a little to myself, then shut up, then just go to pieces and laugh till tears ran down, thinking of Dwight flying through the storm of newspapers. Carla asked me to explain what was so funny. I tried, but couldn't stop laughing. Then she began to laugh, too. She wished she could hear some music and cursed the old truck's lack of a radio. I pulled the tape player out of my wrestling bag and clipped in a special traveling-music tape. She liked that. Then I took out my tea thermos and poured us some. Carla drinks a lot of tea.

"You come prepared," she said.

"I'm just waiting for the day some millionaire will get a flat or run out of gas. I'll change his tire, drive him to a gas station, pour him some tea and honey—and he'll pay my way through college."

"What he'll do is hit you on the head and you'll wake up with an asshole the size of the Chicago Loop." She giggled as I squirmed a bit in fun. "I'm very interested in that bag," she said, looking down at my big old wrestling road bag. "What else do you have in there?"

She was bent over a little and through her second button I could see a nipple register its protest against the cold morning. Her hair was blowing out the window and back against the broken gun rack. God, she looked good driving the old yellow Ford. Among other things it made her freckles redder.

"Oh, I've got a couple pair of socks and some shorts and towels, some soap and a thermos full of Gatorade," I said. I didn't mention Dad's old .9mm Luger.

Carla flipped out when "John Wesley Harding" came on the tape. I knew she liked Bob Dylan because that's what she played all the time on the stereo at the New Pioneer while she drank tea like an addict. I had the tape loaded heavily with Dylan tunes I recorded at Kuch's house. I had some Merle Haggard, some Leon Russell, some New Riders and Grateful Dead, and a couple obscure Jim Croce and John Stewart truck-driving songs. It was definitely a tape for the old Ford on 395 North and for Carla.

We talked about music and books and kids at Lake Shore, Carla's old school in Chicago, and kids at David Thompson. We were laughing so much and having such a good time we forgot to watch the gas gauge. We ran out on the Colville side of Addy and I had to walk back and get some.

More than anything else, I was fascinated with Carla's

independence. There are lots of really beautiful girls around and lots of soft ones who are smiley and bright-eyed and in shape and smell good and don't smoke cigarettes. But I just have the feeling that few of these attractive girls keep time with their own clocks. But Carla had had a baby and she was nineteen and had to be self-sufficient after she left home, so maybe my comparison with the other girls I knew wasn't fair. Anyway, on that trip to the Columbia I was giddy from more than the memory of scaring the pee out of Dwight Thuringer. I was about half in love.

I tried to get her to talk about herself, but all she said was that her father was an insurance executive and her mother was a housefrump, that they were both shit-hooks, and that her brothers and sisters would turn out exactly the same.

"What saved you?" I asked.

"Getting pregnant," she replied.

That sobered me up a little. But just then Dylan's "It Takes a Lot to Laugh, It Takes a Train to Cry" came around on the tape and Carla rocked back and forth and banged on the steering wheel and tapped her free foot in time. The girls I knew were more sedate than that, and right then I realized exactly what it was that fascinated me about Carla. She had the best things I liked about girls and the best things I liked about guys. She was soft and beautiful and made up little animals and could be kind and tender. But she also swore creatively and worked hard at stuff besides her appearance and did what moved her—like leaving home or peeing with the door open or going with a black guy or banging on the steering wheel. Maybe when you get older you begin to appreciate many of the same qualities in the opposite sex that you do in your own. It would be pretty hard to live closely with somebody if you couldn't like her or him at least for the same reasons you liked all your other friends. Now that Carla and I have been together for a while I can feel this happening in me.

We rocked and rolled through the main street of Colville and turned west on 395 to New Kettle Falls and my great-aunt's place on Gold Creek. We talked about our jobs and the jobs we'd had before, laughing about everything. I told Carla about my job helping the Stern family get in shape.

"Last year," I began, "Mr. Stern, a teacher at school, hired me to teach his family an exercise routine that would get them in shape for summer hiking in the Cascades. They're probably on Mt. Rainier right now," I said to add immediacy to the story.

"Umm," Carla replied politely. "What exercises did you teach them?" She was only listening half-intently because the tape had come around to The Dead and "Casey Jones."

"Oh, some pushups and sits and rope skipping and run-a-lap, walk-a-lap. Just stuff everybody already knows. Just stuff to help them build up a little muscle tone. By the end of the year I'd left no Stern untoned."

Not only did Carla refrain from laughing, she didn't even react.

"Stern," I explained. "Stern untoned."

"I'm trying to ignore it," Carla replied. "You are a menace. You scare little paper boys and you make dumb puns. You watch out," she smiled. "You're gonna get it."

"It," of course, was exactly what I wanted.

She talked about working in a record store in Chicago and about all the records she left with her brothers and sisters back home. "It's hard to believe people really live this kind of life," she said, swinging her arm out the window toward the fields and farmhouses. "Nobody next door and nobody across the street. Dogs and cats probably live long enough to die natural deaths here."

"A lot of 'em get killed on the highway," I said. "The more room you've got, the farther you roam." That sounded like a song, so I started to sing it to the tune of "Momma Tried," which was playing at the time. I don't sing nearly as pretty as Merle Haggard, so I shut up after the first few lines.

Carla was mellowing. She was also probably about to have kidney failure from the truck's bouncing. A straight hour of that old Ford suspension was all anybody but a bronc rider could comfortably take. We were almost to Aunt Lola's place, so there wasn't much use to stop and rest. To ease Carla's fluttering kidneys I decided to tell her about the time I introduced the entire Turn family to dope.

"It was shortly after my assignment toning up the Sterns," I began, "that I embarked on my life of crime."

Carla blew a few wisps of hair out of her eyes and looked over at me. "You mugged the milkman," she said.

"Worse," I replied. I looked penitently into my lap and wrung my hands in contrition. I also had a hard-on to conceal. "I led a good middle-American family into intercourse with the evil weed."

"No," Carla said. "Oh, my."

"The Turn family," I continued. "Friends of the Sterns. They wanted to take up hiking, too. They already had muscle tone, but they couldn't stand each other's company long enough to walk together from the davenport to the TV. Mr. Turn came to me one day for help. He saw how I'd brought the Sterns around. It sounded to me like a case of familiarity having bred contempt, so I prescribed alteration in their psychic landscape. I got fifteen fat numbers from Otto and laid them on Mr. Turn, with the instruction to have a boot-oiling and dope-smoking session in the family room while watching a National Geographic special. That was three numbers for each patient. All it took was one apiece before they forgot their boots were warming in the oven. After two they trooped arm-in-arm through the house, singing Sierra Club songs. And after the third they set up camp in the garage and roasted their gerbils over an open fire. They were great friends afterward, even Garret, who had sacrificed his gerb-gerbs for family unity. They had to buy new boots, but Melissa added the roasted shrunken ones to her doll wardrobe. I felt pretty good. After all, I left no Turn unstoned."

I turned to Carla and flashed my biggest grin. Then I pushed out my upper plate with my tongue and let it fall out of my mouth, catching it with lightning speed before it hit the seat.

Carla screamed and almost collided with a logging truck coming from New Kettle. She'd never seen me do that with my teeth before. She drove with her left hand and beat on me with her right. She pulled off in the Gold Creek rest area and beat on me with both fists. I hunched in a ball on the floor and laughed like a loon while Carla pounded away. Then she barked her knuckles on the heater and swore, "Oh, shit, piss, and fuck," and shook her injured fist and began to laugh.

Carla lay across the seat laughing and I sat happily on the floor until I got a muscle spasm in my thigh and couldn't stand it and opened the door and fell out backwards and writhed on the gravel until I rubbed it out. Carla just laughed some more.

After we pulled out of the rest area I could feel things had changed a little between us. For one thing, Carla stopped after she turned off the highway onto Lola's road and gave me a big wet Willy. It was more a playful one than your usual drive-in-movie wet Willy, but it turned me on anyway. She grabbed my head with both hands and lifted my hair and scoured my ear a good one. She must have noticed a strange texture or taste, because she pulled back and scrutinized my ear.

"Louden . . . ?" she began.

"Cauliflower ear," I said. "Both of 'em. Hope it doesn't taste bad."

"It tastes fine," she said, giving me a few softer wet ones. She pulled me over sideways till my head lay on the seat beside her and examined my right ear, which is in a little worse condition than my left. "Don't they hurt?" she asked, after treating my semicircular canals to a generous wash of saliva.

"Only when someone rubs them into the mat," I said.

She thought I was referring to my other ear being mashed into the cracked leather seat, so she let me go and pulled me up and said she was sorry and looked that ear over for damage she might have done. Actually, it had hurt some, but only a little, since my nervous system had been momentarily hijacked by the desperate jolts of sensation rushing to my cock.

We had a great time at Aunt Lola's. We fed the chickens and collected the eggs. We were too late to milk the cow, but we were in time to eat some fresh cream on our breakfast strawberries, which we picked, along with carrots, onions, tomatoes, green beans, corn, and peas. We also dug some spuds and boxed up a few jars of jam and a couple jars of the honey Lola trades eggs to a neighbor for. We mowed the lawn and trimmed it. We cut wood and stacked it. Carla touched me a lot and that reassured me and settled me down. I had gotten pretty excited and nervous thinking about how I could make some moves on her. She was and is more sexually sophisticated than I am. We held hands and walked through the alfalfa to the pond my dad and uncle and cousins had stocked when they were kids. They caught the fish in Gold Creek and ran them down to the pond in buckets. Eastern brook and rainbow grow big in the pond because there's so much food and no kids to catch them any more. We sat on the bank and watched the fish and frogs and water-snakes and turtles go about their business. The pond has grown so green with life I always about half expect to haul in a couple coelacanths or see a trilobite or two squint up at me from the mud. But we didn't fish. We just talked.

We left Lola's at twilight, promising to come back the next day to drive her to Colville so she could do her shopping. I drove and Carla sat on her side of the seat and looked for deer. She'd seen a DEER CROSSING sign and was determined to spot some. She wasn't totally ignoring me, though. As I talked about how the deer come out of the woods in the evenings to feed in the fields, every so often Carla would reach over and let her hand rest on my thigh. She didn't turn to look; she just touched me on the thigh where my jeans were worn thinnest. Sometimes she ran her fingertips along the in-seam. Naturally, I had a raging boner.

We crossed the bridge over Lake Roosevelt and I looked down, but it had gotten too dark to see the level of the water. We drove south and turned off on the road to the Trout Lake campground. I stopped to wire a big can of beef stew to the exhaust manifold so it would be warm for our dinner. We took off for the campground, and rounding the first curve, we hit a little doe. She must have been standing just on the shoulder of the road, because she jumped square into our right fender. If she'd been very far off the road, she'd have jumped clean over us. It scared Carla because it happened so fast and about two feet from her nose. And it scared me because I had been talking about how I learned to heat canned food on the exhaust manifolds of the trucks and dozers at the Trapper Peak forest fire and wasn't paying much attention to my driving.

The little doe lay in the ditch in front of us crying and kicking the two legs that weren't broken. People think deer don't make sounds, but they do. They sort of whistle. Her eyes were wild and she shook her head from side to side and tried to get up. The hide was barked on her face and shoulder, but aside from that she looked okay. Except for her two right legs, which only swept a little gravel, no matter how she thrashed away. "Poor little deer," I said. I don't mind killing animals—to eat, for example. But I sure can hardly stand to see them suffer, or people either.

Carla didn't know much about deer, or at least not wild deer, so when she went close to pet her and comfort her a little, the doe kicked out with a good leg and raked Carla's arm. She yelled and jumped back in surprise and then got another surprise when she looked down and saw her shirt torn and her arm bleeding. Deer hooves are very sharp and not all that clean. I sat Carla down on the running board and looked at her arm. I had to get a flashlight to see. The cut was shallow, but about an inch wide. The skin was ripped down the inside of her arm from her elbow to the middle of her forearm. A four-inch flap of it hung in her shirt sleeve.

"I just wanted to pet it," Carla said.

"I know," I said. "Me, too. But she can't know."

"Isn't there some way we can help her?" Carla asked. "She's crying."

I cut Carla's sleeve off with my hunting knife and pulled the skin flap back over the cut and wrapped her arm in gauze. "I'd like to wash this," I said, not answering her question. "But all we have is Gatorade."

"And you're saving it to drink," she replied.

"Damn right," I said.

66

"Can't we keep her from suffering?" Carla asked.

"I'm gonna shoot her."

"But she only has broken legs. And she's a deer, not a racehorse."

"I know," I said. "But she'll starve. Somebody'll come along and shoot her, anyway."

"You don't have a gun," Carla said.

"It's in my bag."

"Please do it now, then," she said. "It's awful to hurt alone."

So I got the Luger and walked behind the deer and shot her once through the back of the head. She shook with the impact of the bullet, but then she went still and didn't twitch at all. The shot rang and rang in my ears, that gun is so loud.

I let down the tailgate and shoved the dead deer in with her head hanging out so she wouldn't drip blood on our stuff when we went downhill. At the campground we gave her to the ranger and I washed Carla's arm and found out the nearest doctor was back in Kettle. The ranger couldn't do any more for the cut than I could, but he did promise to hold a camp spot for us if we wanted to come back. Carla said we did and we took off, barreling down the gravel road to the highway. I wanted to get there fast so maybe the doctor could stitch the skin back on.

It turned out the cut wasn't very bad after all. The lady doctor just called it a "scrape" and snipped off the flap of skin, cleaned the grit out, and gave Carla a tetanus shot. We talked a little and she gave us Rocky Mountain spotted fever shots for free. We just had to pay for the tetanus toxoid, and it was only $3.50.

The ride back to Trout Lake was beautiful. The night was warm and clear. We drove real slow and there were lots of falling stars. When we crossed over to the west side of the river we saw lots of deer and a couple porcupines. When we got to the campground the ranger had the doe dressed out and hanging from a hook at the side of his house. Carla couldn't use her arm much, so I set up the tent alone. She went right to sleep after we ate the stew, but I talked to some of the folks camping around us, and to the ranger to see if he'd seen anything of my grandpa.

I crawled into the tent then and lay for a few minutes on top of my sleeping bag looking at the dark silhouette of Carla lying on her side in her sleeping bag. I reached up and traced along her hip lightly with my finger; then I pulled off my T-shirt and jeans and crawled into the bag, where I fought the desire to beat off until the birds began to sing.

Carla got up early and watched some Canadians fish off the bank for a while, she said, before she woke me. I took down the tent, stowed it, fired up the Ford, and headed us for the highway. We were silent for a while, just looking out through the big Ponderosa pines at Trout Lake sparkling in the clear morning. Then I asked, "Carla, did you smell that beautiful smell this morning? I've never smelled anything like that in the woods before."

She turned from her window and looked at me, then turned back. "Dip," she said. "You were sleeping with your nose in my panties. You drooled on them."

"Sorry," was all I could think to say, and we rode in silence to Barney's Junction for breakfast.

Barney's is on the west side of the Columbia, right where 395 crosses and heads north along the river for a short way before it meets the Kettle River and follows it into Canada. Barney's is to the loggers and farmers and mill workers who live along the river what The Shack is to the car-business people in Spokane. We pulled in, got some gas, and stood looking at the river. And it really was a river. It was lower than I'd ever seen it, low as I'd hoped it would be. I felt like running across the highway and down the bank to stand beside it, but I controlled myself. We'd planned to eat breakfast, and I wanted to catch my grandfather before he left for the day and ask him if he'd like to drive down and visit the falls with us.

"Mornin'," I said to the waitress as she looked us over for signs of California hippiness. "Say," I said, "we're up from Spokane, looking for my grandfather, Harry Swain. Has he been around?"

"Harry was in here yesterday," she said smiling. "You're not Bert's boy?" Bert is my uncle.

"No," I said. "I'm Louden, Larry's boy."

"Larry's boy!" she said. "I thought Larry'd be a grand-father by now."

"Not that any of us knows of." I smiled real big. "How did Harry look?"

"Got a gut on him," she said. "But he's lookin' a lot better lately."

"That's good," I said. Rural people are a little nicer to you if they know you have some local roots.

That was late August and absolutely the last time I could rationalize eating like a regular human being. I told myself I'd chow down until we got back home. And chow down I did: ham and eggs, a chocolate malt, and hot apple pie with cinnamon sauce and ice cream. I weighed 165. If I looked a plate of ham and eggs in the eye right now, my stomach wouldn't even growl in recognition, it's been so long.

"This ham is incredible," Carla said.

"Look at the eggs," I said. "Look at the color of the yolks."

"They're a lot darker," she affirmed.

"That comes from chickens what gets exercise," I said through the deep golden yolk in my mustache. Egg yolk can really give body to a sparse mustache. "Chickens what eats gravel and bugs. Chickens what lives in chicken yards and not no little cages." I had become pretty rural in my excitement to get down to the river.

We caught Grandpa Harry just as he was leaving. I saw the old green jeep pulling onto the highway, so I laid on the horn. We turned onto his road and stopped right beside him.

"I'll be damned," he said and laughed. He always laughs when he first sees me. It's as though it's wondrous to him that I can make it all the way up from Spokane by myself. "What you doin' around here?"

"Dad read the river was comin' down, so we came up to take a look. Thought you might like to drive down to the falls with us. This is Carla," I said. "Carla, this is my grandfather, Harry Swain."

"Pleased to make your acquaintance," Grandpa Harry said.

Carla leaned over me and stuck her good arm out the window and shook with Harry. "My pleasure," she said. Harry thought that was funny as hell. You could see him laughing all the way as he backed up into his yard.

I don't know if it's possible, but it seemed as though he was shorter than when we went fishing together at the start of summer. When my dad was a kid, Harry was supposed to have been a little over six feet. But walking behind him to the cabin, I was a good two fingers taller, and I'm only five-eleven. Carla was searching through the junked cars by the creek, where we saw a couple cats go running. Harry unlocked the padlock on his door and we went in. He just has a hole in the wall and a hole in his door and a chain to go through them. I sat on the floor and leaned against the stove and studied the guns and fish poles in the gun rack, as I always do. Harry took a Medihaler out of his shirt pocket and gave himself a couple good blasts down the throat. He breathed deep through his mouth and smiled.

"They give me these down t' the Vets," he said. "I can fish, hunt, hike these goddamn mountains—anything I want. I just carry a couple of these along. I might even feel like doin' some rasslin'," he said and laughed until the crap in his lungs crackled and snapped like a wood fire. He moved his hands like he was milking a cow and rose about two inches off the bed, as though he were going to come for me.

"Go find yourself some Indian woman to wrestle with," I said. "You'd just hurt me, and this is my year to be a hero."

"A hero . . . !" He laughed and coughed up a few cubic centimeters of trench warfare and spit it in his spitcan alongside the bed. It's a good thing he got his emphysema in the war and not just from his home-land air. This way he's got the Veterans' Hospital any-time he needs it and he's got his pension. The State of Washington lets him hunt and fish for free now that he's over seventy-five, and Dad finds him a cheap old jeep or a pickup when the one he's got goes too bad for any of us to fix.

"How 'bout it?" I asked. "Comin' down to the falls with us?"

"Naw," Harry said. "I'm gonna run up to Davis Lake an' fish."

"We could see the old homestead."

"That place is just a dirty old ditch to me," Harry said. "Goin' fishin'."

Just then Carla came in holding a dusty yellow cat and sat in the chair.

71

"Gonna have some fleas in all them red curls," Grandpa Harry said.

"That's okay," Carla replied, scratching the cat's head and sending it into ecstasy. "Couldn't be more than I get sitting next to him." And she pointed at me.

Harry loved that. He laughed and spit again, but just tobacco this time. Carla didn't bat an eyelash. Harry told her she oughta know better than pet deer like they was dogs and cats, and Carla said she'd remember.

We sat for a few minutes talking about which creeks were fished out and who had been snakebit and how sparse the deer would be come fall. We refused several coffee offers and finally I said we'd better get moving so we could see the falls and take Aunt Lola to Colville to do her grocery shopping. I asked Grandpa Harry if he needed anything. I don't know what I could do for him, but Dad always asks, so I do, too.

"Shit," he said, getting up and walking us out the door. "I don't need nothin'. Got these inhalers and I'll prob'ly be dead before I know it and then I won't even need them no more."

Carla set the cat down by the porch and we walked across the little bit of grass to the truck. I ground the gears and Harry laughed and pointed and said something I couldn't hear. We waved and I honked and Grandpa Harry waved his hand back at us. The cat rubbed his boot top and he gave it a gentle shove off the porch. Then he laughed some more and touched two fingers to the brim of his straw fishing hat and stuck out his arm and waved again before he went to work chaining his door.

"What will he do?" Carla asked as we turned onto the highway.

"He'll drive up to Davis Lake and fish and shoot

snakes,' I said. And I honked a few final times and looked up the bank to see if he was standing there.

Carla and I drove back to Barney's, crossed the bridge, and turned onto the dirt road that leads to the public access. The sun was high by then and the cheatgrass was dry. Grasshoppers zinged through the air and banged into the sides of the pickup. A dull roar like the rumble of heavy trucks rose ahead of us. It grew into a real thunder as we crested the last hill before the road dropped down to the riverbank. We stopped a minute and looked out. The scene was about the same as I remembered it from ten or so years before and about the same as I dream it now. Where fat lazy Lake Roosevelt had lain in a bed of sand, the Columbia River cut through rock. Northward lay the mudflat that had once been farmland. An olive-drab Dodge Power Wagon was skidding driftwood logs through the mud to dry ground. Its driver and Carla and I were the only folks around.

We walked down the rocky trail, across the dry sandy beach, through wet sand, and finally through mud before we reached the boulders that gleamed through the driftwood and trash. It looked like a whole lakeful of litter had lodged where the channel narrowed. The heat drew a dead smell from the mud. Carla walked back to the clean sand to lie in the sun while I worked my way across the rocks and logs to a broad ledge parallel to the falls but higher in elevation and about thirty yards away. White plastic bleach jugs floated in the shallow pools and hung like snowberries in the driftwood jams.

I sat on the wet rock, drew my arms around my knees, and gazed south. Thin and blue, the river rolled through a black band of mud bordered by white sand. Where the white sand ended, green pines rose and blurred in the distance to dark high-mountain blue. On the east ran the Huckleberry Mountains and on the west the Kettle River Range. Some of the land between the mountain ranges south to the great bend in the river still belongs to the Spokane and Colville Indian tribes.

I felt insulated by the roar of water all around me. I couldn't hear the cars on the highway, and when I closed my eyes I couldn't see the trash.

I was thinking of something Seattle, Chief of the Duwamish Indians, had said about his people and their land on Puget Sound:

> When the last red man shall have perished, and the memory of my tribe shall have become a myth among the white man, these shores will swarm with the invisible dead of my tribe. . . . they will throng with the returning hosts that once filled and still love this beautiful land.

I was thinking of those invisible dead and of my own as I pulled the cassette recorder from my wrestling bag and set it on the rock ledge. A shower of mist blew off the falls and with it fell a great coolness. I watched the tiny points of moisture brighten the black surface of the machine for a second before I pressed "record."

When I got back to the clean part of the beach I found Carla sunning with her shirt off. She opened one eye as she heard my footsteps squinch across the sand. I was slightly crazed by the river, I guess, or I wouldn't have had the nerve to do what I did then. I stood above her and let myself topple from the ankles like a tree. She yelped, but I caught myself before I touched her. My head level with her breasts, I did one pushup kissing her right nipple and another pushup kissing her left. Then my nerve deserted me and I got up and ran like hell for the pickup.

"Wait!" I heard Carla yell behind me.

Aunt Lola was sitting in the rocking chair on her porch waiting for us when we arrived. Since my great-uncle Walker died Lola has had to depend on family and friends for some little things, like splitting wood and rides into New Kettle and Colville. She said the Baptist church van comes around once a week to take folks into town and back, but that she can't always catch it because she doesn't always feel up to walking out to the highway. I don't know the name of the condition that makes old peoples' ankles swell—maybe it's just Time—but whatever it is, her ankles get about the size of cantaloupes, so it's no wonder she doesn't feel like walking out to the highway.

We had a good ride. The past year and a half or so, Lola and most of the other folks, young and old, around what they call "Panorama Land" have been pretty upset about all the "hippies" moving in and marring the panorama. Communes spring up around Colville like toadstools around Lola's pond.

"There's another one a them hippy girls," Lola said of what I took to be a normally overdressed girl walking down the main street in a sunbonnet, shawl, long dress, and bare feet. "At least she looks clean."

We teased her some. "Prob'ly nothin' but a mass a marijuana scabs under that dress," I said.

"Her packsack is probably full of food stamps and Goodwill underwear," Carla said.

"Well, she don't look no worse than the two of you." Lola smiled at us. And boy, was she correct.

"You know," I said, "I've seen pictures of you and Uncle Walker where you looked just about like that girl there and Walker had a handlebar mustache about to his ears. You're a lot prettier than that girl, of course," I added, giving her a little elbow in the ribs.

It's easy to forget sometimes that people Lola's age were raising families before cars were a common thing, were grandparents before a jet first broke the sound barrier, and now buy Skylab and lunar module toys for Christmas presents. I think it speaks well of my Aunt Lola that she even took a ride in the pickup with Carla and me without pushing money on us for haircuts and new jeans.

In the Safeway store I gave Carla a small kiss on the back of her neck when she bent down to sniff the smoked salmon in the meat bin, and she goosed me with a big purple beet in the vegetable aisle. Then she got me with another wet Willy as I balanced a twenty-five-pound bag of sugar on my head to the check stand. Later, back on the lawn at Lola's, I countered by lifting her in the air over my head and blowing fierce and wet in her belly button. Then I pretended to take a long time getting the lint out of my mouth.

"Louden!" Lola yelled from the door. "You're too big to be handling her that way. You'll have her other arm all cut up soon."

I growled something brutish in gorilla language.

"Help! Help!" chirped Carla.

"Carla, you don't let him play like that while he's driving. You'll have a wreck." And Lola waved a slab of bacon at us and turned for the kitchen.

"I'll make him ride in back!" Carla yelled, catching me off guard and shoulder-blocking me over the lawn mower flat onto a rhubarb plant.

"Aunt Lola!" I yelled. "Can we take enough rhubarb home for a pie?"

"Look," I said to Carla when we were almost out of Colville on the way headed home. "Why don't we stay another night? I don't have to work until three-thirty tomorrow afternoon. We could camp out on the Little Pend Oreille and have dinner at this big old lodge up there."

"I'll call Belle and ask her to work tomorrow morning for me," Carla replied.

We found a great campsite right away beneath some cedars just a few feet from the water.

If Carla hadn't opened both sleeping bags and spread them out in the tent we might never have made love. I had cut wood and stacked it for the evening and had begun to identify birds, plants, trees, small animals, and had started on the clouds in the sky when she said, "Louden, why don't we just lie down a while?"

She took off her shirt and bundled it up for a pillow and lay back in the red haze that the sunlight made through the red nylon tent. She didn't have much of a tan, really, so she looked pearly in all that soft red light with the bushels of red hair spilled around her head and her nipples sprung up like small flowers. She smiled calmly and turned on her side. I took off my shirt and boots and lay beside her. And then she said, "Let's wait a long time." So we did.

We were slick with sweat and slipping around the wet sleeping-bag floor like happy seals.

"The reason I want to play a long time," Carla finally said, "is that this will be the first time I've made love since I had my baby, and I'm not sure how it's going to feel."

"How's it feel so far?" I asked.

"It feels fine," she said.

I didn't believe her about it being the first time since she'd had her baby. I just assumed she'd been making it with Tower, since she spent so much time with him. But I didn't know if I should say anything. Finally I did.

"You don't have to say that about your love-making," I said. "It doesn't matter." It came out sounding like I was forgiving her for something, but I really just wanted her to know I was willing to accept her on her own terms.

77

"I haven't been making love with Austin," she said. "First I was too sore and then I wasn't sure and then his girl friend came all the way from New York. Girls don't spend time with guys just to get laid," she said.

I admit it, hearing her say it made me feel good.

We lay a little longer, just touching and kissing slowly. Carla definitely set the pace those first times. What she was doing was teaching me how she liked it to be. And then she looked me square in the eye and said, "You can do anything you want to me."

That sentence I had heard so often in the final throes of wet dreams, had so often fantasized in the last quick strokes of a bathroom beat-off break at school, that sentence opening the way for travel in the farthest reaches of the erotic cosmos had a strange effect: my cock wilted like a sunflower on a gray day.

I rose again, but only after I had confessed my awe at the grandeur of her invitation and after Carla had shown me some of my options.

I never really thought I'd ever come head to head with the prospect of fulfilled fantasy. She talked about everything in sex being beautiful if it felt good and said she thought everything would feel wonderful with a guy as gentle as me. That was a very nice thing for her to say and it made me feel awful good. I told her I had some pretty violent but friendly feelings about the love I'd like to make to her and that I'd never felt that way before. Then everything was all right and we proceeded to fuck around and around, rolling and intertwining like two weasels with one lame paw.

Carla, having a few violent feelings of her own, pulled my hair and bit me little hard ones and dug her fingers into me all over. Thank Christ she keeps her fingernails short. I squeezed her till her vertebrae cracked and drove into her with all my abdominal strength, which is a lot even in the off-season. Carla laid her head back and made beautiful animal sounds. I tried to pull out, but she held me and told me to "come, come," that she was taking pills. I came and came, all right. I also twitched like a freshly killed snake and gasped like a victim of cardiac collapse. I had never experienced any feeling like that before. It was several universes beyond any pleasure I'd even imagined. Hard as I worked to help her, Carla didn't come. But she did say she liked the love. Now that we've had some practice she comes all the time.

When we reestablished our relationship with the world outside the two of us, we found ourselves in a red twilight. Carla peeked outside and then turned back and said, "Nobody's around. Let's go for a swim."

"That water is cold," I informed her.

"Think how good it will feel." And she rubbed her hands together, gave me a quick kiss on my shriveled peter, and burst bare-assed through the tent flaps. I heard a splash and then a scream. Then, "Oh, God, it's wonderful!" That water was so cold it drove my testes up about to my spleen. But it truly was wonderful.

Later, at the lodge, Carla looked up from her dinner and around at all the people and up at the deer, elk, bear, bobcat, pheasant, and fish trophies on the walls and turned back to me and said, "We have a secret. We know something nobody else in here knows."

Actually, I thought our secret was showing. Carla glowed like sunset and I couldn't stop the smiles coming. We couldn't keep our hands off each other. And maybe it was just the fragrance remaining in my mustache, but in spite of our icy creek baths, I thought we smelled like a fish sack left out in the sun.

"And we're going to have another one when we get back to the tent," Carla said.

We've been having secrets like that ever since.

IX

I'm lying on a cot. Tanneran is sitting on a stool talking to me. He says I fainted dead away when I got up to give my book report. He says we walked down here to the nurse's office and I seemed okay until I fainted again. I feel like I just sprinted to the top of Mt. Rainier and went takedowns with a Sasquatch.

"How's your weight?" Gene asks.

"Forty-seven last night," I reply.

"Did you have any breakfast?"

"A veritable feast, Gene. A big bowl of Carla's yogurt with some giant chunks of fresh pineapple."

"What'd you do before class?" Gene asks.

"I skipped my two study halls and did a workout," I reply slowly.

"What sort of workout?" Gene's being very slow with me. I'm grateful. I'm having a little trouble following.

"Regular workout, Gene," I say. "I ran three. Did five hundred pushups, a hundred dips, a thousand sits."

Gene shakes his head. "And what did you weigh then?"

"Forty-six."

"I'll bet anything you're going down too fast," Gene says. He purses his lips and nods. "Coach is on his way. He'll know."

"Where's the nurse? Where's the damn nurse?" Coach flaps his arms, looking in all directions.

"She doesn't come on Fridays," I hear myself whisper. I feel strange.

"What do you weigh?" Coach asks. I close my eyes and breathe through my mouth. My fingertips tingle and my body seems to float. I can't feel the gray wool blanket I know I'm lying on. In my mind I see Coach waving at me from the top of David Thompson's green and gold water tower in the park. He's yelling toward school, where I'm being kept prisoner. I think he wants to spring me, but I can hardly hear.

Gene answers for me. "Forty-six after a workout about fifteen minutes ago." Gene's voice is far away.

"Christ!" Coach rants. "He's going down way too fast. He's probably dehydrated. I'll go get some salt. Make him drink some water, Gene." And Coach is gone.

I hear his heels click. He's walking right down the side of the water tower! What balance! Boy, I'd have hated to wrestle Coach Ratta in his prime.

I lose control. I rave. I'm out the window, up the hill in the park. It's summer and I'm swinging on the big kids' swing. I throw my head back and pump for the sky. Upside-down a green and gold kingdom oscillates feudally. There are 2563 of us in David Thompson High School. That's more than some small towns. The high school is green and gold, the junior high, the grade school, the water tower, the public toilet, the grass, the sun. I swing level with the bar. I stretch my head way back, the ground swooshing, swooshing in my ears. I can't get sick now. I always get sick on the big swing. I look down. How many David Thompson sneakers rubbed to sand this former grass? My teeth fall out. They slide across the sandy patch below, near, then very far as I swing. They nip the iron pole, bite down on a clump of grass. I can't get sick now. I'm lean. I carry the colors of the Columbia. I can make the river flow again. My short hair brushes the sand, the grass, the sand, the grass. My nose begins to bleed, arcing dots of blood elliptically. I rave. I jump.

Gene catches me. He's making me drink water. It's easy, because I'm thirsty as hell.

"You're all right, man," Gene says. "You're just dehydrated."

"Victim of a fucked-up nitrogen balance," I reply. "At least I hope that's all, Gene. There's no end to the terrible diseases people can get." I've been reading *Rare Diseases* lately. It's ghastly. Poe could have written it.

I feel a bit better. Things have changed a little since Gene wrestled in high school back in the middle sixties. I explain to him how I've got to have a doctor's permission to drop down to 147. I have my appointment next Tuesday, the day after Christmas. The appointment's in the morning; then we wrestle Lewis and Clark in the afternoon. If I'm much over fifty, I doubt the old doctor will let me go down. We have to wrestle eight matches at the weight we'll wrestle in the state tournament. Outside of those eight, we can wrestle in any class above the one we start the season in. But if we want to drop down a class, then we have to have a doctor's permission. I wrestled my first match this season at sixty-five; then I dropped to fifty-four. I'll wrestle at fifty-four against Lewis and Clark Tuesday afternoon, then once or maybe twice more in the Custer-Battleground meet in Missoula next Friday and

Saturday. Then Shute at 147 on the day after New Year's. Coach is back, stuffing yellow salt tablets down me.

"Salt," he says.

"Sodium depletion," I reply.

"You're crazy," Coach says. "Shute'll take you apart if you ruin your health going down too fast."

"My doctor's appointment's Tuesday," I say.

"You'll be all right if you stay about fifty, fifty-one. Take salt. Don't start dehydrating. And don't screw so much, for Chrissake!" Then Coach pounds me on the chest, knocking the wind out of me, and clicks off down the hall.

I feel a lot better after I get my breath. I'm hungry. I remember I haven't mentioned Carla. Coach just gave me a good opportunity. I'm a little weak yet, but I think fast.

"God," I moan. "A guy can deny himself only just so many needs of the flesh. I'm not sure willpower would do it, anyway. I think all this weight loss has given me priapism. The problem may be pathological, Gene."

"Priapism?" Gene says. I can see him thinking, Priapism? Priapism? What the fuck is priapism? Gene knows a lot of stuff, but sometimes I can catch him.

"A disease of constant hard-on," I explain. "I'll bet Coach wouldn't tell Carla to slack off. She'd gouge his eyes, invert his navel." I'm getting in pretty good spirits.

"Carla!" Gene exclaims quietly. "I thought you and she didn't get along. What happened to the black dude?"

Tower used to take Carla to the Spokes' games. About half the time Gene didn't know the snap, he'd be scouting the bleachers so intently for beaver. He used to love to dive for sideline tackles so he could roll under the bleachers and look up skirts.

"Gene, kind of a sad thing happened to that relationship. One day last August this black girl walked into

Tower's apartment and began to shout at Carla how she is his old lady come from New York and that Carla had best get her little red-haired ass out of there in a big hurry. Carla knows just what to do if people are leering at her, but she doesn't react well at all to threats of physical violence. Carla grabbed onto Tower and this girl started pulling her off. Tower got between them and told Carla she'd better split. So Carla did. She doesn't talk about it much. Elmo's the one who told me. Carla and I get along pretty well now."

"I'll be damned," Gene says.

"Listen," I say. "How would you like to meet one of Carla's friends? She's better-looking than Carla—a little flashier. Her chromosomes are probably restructured, but she's a nice girl."

"What's her name?" Gene asks.

"Belle," I reply.

Gene nods his head. I'm sure he's seen her around. Everybody knows cheerleaders.

X

We're circled up on the mat and Coach is going over the scouting report for the Lewis and Clark match. L.C. is especially tough in the lower weights. Damon Thuringer, "Sausage Man," our sophomore at 105, has a real tough one. He's wrestling a Japanese kid named Kenuchi Mashamura. Mash is a senior who has taken the state championship at both 119 and 112. Early in the season a *Spokesman Review* article quoted him as saying he was beginning to think seriously about college wrestling, so he thought he'd train real hard this season and drop down to a weight where he could be more competitive. He was sincere. He's a very humble guy. He's also a monster, a real teratoid. He looks about thirty years old with his giant little body and his furry eyebrows and cauliflower ears even more grotesque than mine. Of course, Mash is undefeated.

Sausage is a baby-faced, flute-playing, downy-haired Hobbit. Carla thinks he's the cutest thing in the world and is always after me to stop scaring his little brother.

Sausage's record is four and four. He is well-conditioned and fierce to a fault, but I hope he's made peace with himself. Coach has made him captain for the meet. That'll help a little. It always gives the guy a psychological boost. The whole school knows who the captain is because Coach announces it over the intercom at the beginning of the week. Kids encourage him in the halls, call him "Captain" and stuff. And when he leads us out on the mat and circles us up for our warm-ups, people ooh and aah and yell heartening sentiments because they know what a tough match the guy must have if he's captain.

As we're circled here on the mat listening to Coach go over the scouting report, Otto and I plot to harass the Sausage Man.

Coach is saying he's glad Kuch and I got our wrestle-off for Shute out of the way a few days early, so now we can get down to thinking about the immediate future. We could have waited until next week, but we were too nervous and wanted to get it done. I'm glad we did. Before, I was worried about Kuch and Shute. Now I'm just worried about Shute. Both Kuch and I still officially have to wrestle off with our number-two men to see who wrestles L.C. But we've been beating them all season.

While Coach explains that Kuch's man likes to work a fireman's carry right to a fast pin, Otto and I sneak around the circle to Sausage, who peers out from beneath a pile of wool blankets. He has some trouble making weight. He's down from 125 as a cross-country man. He spends slack time doing pushups and situps in his rubber sweat suit under his bunch of wool blankets. You'll come off the mat after a drill and off in a corner will be a boy-sized green heap with gold trim pumping furiously up and down. We often wonder aloud about the true nature of these movements. It's reported that his girl is denying Sausage his strokes and that Sausage has taken to throbbing his cob more frequently than may be healthy.

Otto sneaks one way and I sneak the other. Coach is talking about Romaine Lewis, L.C.'s man at fifty-four. Coach looks around for me. I stop my stealthy crawl and pop up behind Kenny Schmoozler, our man at 133. Carla thinks Schmoozler's name is awfully cute. She says that with a name like that, Schmoozler should be a little animal. I assure her that he is.

"Lewis will take you down, you let yourself get weak!" Coach yells.

"I feel great, Coach." I gleam. "That Romaine Lettuce is a doper. He won't take me down. I'll dance, sing, dice him, slice him. I'll counsel him on the dangers of snorting hair straightener. His internal environment is polluted. Lettuce won't take me down."

Coach covers his eyes. He knows when the team is feeling right.

"Did you eat?" he growls.

"I ate, I ate. Two carob bars and a can of Nutrament," I reply. "Lean and mean, Coach! Lean and mean!" I chant.

Otto snorts like a wild pig. "Lean and mean, lean and mean!" He's worked his way around to Sausage and kicks him through his blankets.

"Lean and mean! Lean and mean!" the Sausage Man pipes.

Now all of us are rooting around the mats on all fours, bumping into each other, grunting like frenzied swine, chanting, "Lean and mean! Lean and mean!"

Coach lets us go for about a minute, then continues with the scouting report. We stop. We've got to conserve. There's a tough practice ahead.

Otto and I sit with our arms resting on Thuringer. He

peeks his head out at Otto, then leers at me. "Don't fuck with me," the Sausage Man warns.

"Damon," I say. "Damon, my boy. Otto and I have only come to congratulate you on your captaincy."

"Bite ass, Swain," Sausage says. "Just bite ass."

Otto is offended by this unfriendliness. He tweaks Sausage's nose and pushes his head under the blankets.

"Sausage Man," Otto coos. "We know what you do under your blankies. No more hacking your lizard in the privacy of your little nest. Self-abuse saps your strength, Sausage. Take heed: thou shalt not pump thy pepperoni."

"You fuckers better not hurt my lip. I haven't got my mouthpiece," Sausage informs us. Being a good flute player, Sausage really has to take care of his lip.

"Your mouthpiece is in a safe place, Damon," I reply.

The Sausage Man groans from beneath his blankets. He knows where that safe place is. Every chance I get I stuff his mouthpiece down my jock. He's usually more careful with it. He must be worried about his match. He left it on the windowsill.

Coach is demonstrating to Jean-Pierre Baldosier, our number-one man at 185, how his L.C. man likes to stack people up with a double chicken wing. We call him "Balldozer" half out of fun and respect for the way he munches people and about half because we can't pronounce his name right.

Coach's arms are hooked deeply under Jean-Pierre's armpits, and Coach has driven him forward on the mat so that his neck has bent underneath him and he is now "stacked up" on his shoulders, his feet waving in the air. Coach asks if Balldozer understands the move. Balldozer can't breathe, let alone speak, and he tries to communicate that idea with gasps and grunts. Coach thinks he's requesting further demonstration, so he reefs some more

88

on the double chicken wing. Balldozer is pinned. His scapulae rest on the mat. His nose is buried in his hairy chest. Coach cinches up good on his chicken wing, scrunching Jean-Pierre even further into the shape of an upside-down question mark, and asks again if he understands. Taking advantage of Coach's inattention, Otto flops down on Sausage, who is mashed from lump to patty. He squeals unintelligibly. Otto watches attentively as Balldozer's head turns purple and blue, while I reach under the blankets and pull off Sausage's shoes and socks.

Coach is finished with Balldozer, who gasps and nods that he understands about the double-chicken-wing-stackup series.

Coach waives comment on Otto's L.C. man in favor of some brief predictions about the damage the Montana heavyweights are likely to do him when we travel there next Friday. Coach isn't kidding. Those cowpokers really can be mean.

"Cowboys and miners!" Otto giggles, trembling in mock fear.

Behind him I stuff two sweat socks in Thuringer's mouth, being careful not to damage his lip. Then I begin to tie his head between his knees with his shoelaces. I finish just as Coach does, and we all jump up to begin the exercises. All except the Sausage Man. We quickly heave him deep in his favorite corner and cover him up good.

We're in our warm-up lines and Coach opens his mouth to scream the first exercise at us when a light but persistent knocking sounds at the door.

Coach screams at the knocking and the door opens hesitantly, revealing red curls. It's Carla.

Coach points at me and points at the door. Coach knows of my semimarital state. Carla babysits Coach's kids sometimes. I trot over. Behind me Coach screams, "On your backs! Neck drill!"

I hear the flops and grunts and straining as the guys bridge on their necks, navels ceilingward, hands pounding bellies. The chanting starts, a steady "ahhhhhhhhhhhhhh" in time with the pounding hands. A simple tribal song, the sound of clean lungs. I close the door on this familiar rumbling and see that Carla is worried.

"What's wrong?" I ask.

"I heard you fainted in class," she says. "Are you okay?"

"Okay," I say. "Just a little light-headed."

"You should have let me know you were all right," Carla says sternly.

"I'm sorry. I didn't even think that someone might tell you," I reply. "I'm sorry—really!" I repeat, going close to kiss her.

Carla's worry has changed to mild pissed-offness. We kiss and part. She sniffs. She moves close again and sniffs my sweat clothes. She wilts, swoons. I lean her against the wall.

"That smell is not human," she gasps, rubbing her eyes and wrinkling her nose.

Carla pinches the cloth of my sweat shirt delicately, as though she were examining the texture of a turd. The salt crystals crinkle lightly beneath her fingertips. "Ouhhh!" she says with a grimace. "Don't you ever wash this stuff?" This is Carla's first trip up to the wrestling room. She must be skipping her child development class.

"Of course not," I reply indignantly. "You wash practice sweats before the season starts and that's it," I explain. "Each time you put them on you're reminded of all the fat you sweated out the day before. You can feel it. Besides, the smell deadens your mucous membranes, reducing the occurrence of bloody nose. Much healthier than cocaine."

My good spirits persist in spite of my light-headedness, maybe even aided by the condition. But Carla isn't having any of my jive.

"Does everyone do it that way?" she asks, cringing away.

"Not everyone," I reply. "Mostly just Otto and Kuch and Schmoozler and me—we're the seasoned veterans."

"Jesus," Carla retorts. "You should be seasoned. You should be pickled from wearing this stuff."

The team is past pushups and into sits now. "Stick your head in and take a whiff," I encourage her.

She does. "Glaaah!" She retches, slamming the door. "It's like ammonia. You can feel it in the air. Eyccch!" She shimmies and hops, wiping her nose on her pinafore. "It's on me!" she shrieks.

I laugh.

"I'll pick you up at a quarter after," Carla says, starting down the stairs.

I lean down after her and pooch my lips out for a kiss. "Glaaah!" She shudders and flees.

Behind me I hear the team running in place, the tiny rapid steps, the chant going strong. I'll miss the wrestling room, stuck up here in the rafters of the gym. I'll miss climbing the stairs, throwing Kuch's headgear out the window at basketball players, hiding Sausage's mouthpiece in my jock. I'll miss the air, so full of sweat it stings. The walls dripping with it. Coach keeps the wrestling room at eighty degrees. We've got mats wall to wall and five feet up the sides so nobody gets smashed into the concrete. Now that the team is so big we have to do our drills in shifts. Coach won't cut anybody. Every guy who comes to practice gets to be on the team. If he's the best he gets to wrestle number one varsity. If he's second best he gets to wrestle number two varsity or number one junior varsity. If he's third best he gets to wrestle number one JV or number two JV. It depends on how tough the matches are and how bad the team needs to win. Coach remembers when he had to go through the halls grabbing guys, asking them if they wanted to turn out for the wrestling team. After we won the state championship last year, the PTA wanted to build us a new wrestling room. Otto and Schmooz and Kuch and I had to threaten to move to Moses Lake before they'd leave us alone.

I slip through the door and find myself some moving room. Soon I'm lost in the thunder.

We're about to begin our wrestle-offs. Coach walks to a corner of the wrestling room to watch. Coach never referees the wrestle-offs or participates in any way. Guys who aren't wrestling at the time do all the refereeing. We all know Coach has his favorites among us, but it's not Coach's opinion that determines the first team. In wrestling, unlike football or basketball, there's none of this crap about how good so-and-so looked in practice. If a wrestler beats everybody in his weight class, he's number one. That's all there is to it. In wrestle-offs Coach roots for nobody. Coach walks to a corner and takes a seat on a pile of green and gold blankets. I look across the room at Otto, whose big face contorts into giggles. We're about to have a diversion.

Coach sits down and his face immediately goes quizzical. He bends his head between his legs and lifts the blankets a bit to check the source of the tremors he feels. Coach finds he is sitting on the Sausage Man.

Untied, Sausage leaps up and down and spits all over. He has this tendency to spit when he gets excited. He's like a lawn sprinkler when he plays his flute. If you're in the audience you've either got to stand way back or wear a raincoat. I doubt the problem is pathological.

Sausage pulls his headgear on sideways and gets his nose stuck in an ear hole. He rips it off and flings it at Otto, who convulses in the center of the mat. "Fucking lardass Lafte!" the Sausage spits.

I pull his mouthpiece out of my jock and toss it to him gently.

"Fucking Swain!" he slavers. "You muscle-bound dog turd!"

Sausage spits lint and chunks of sweat sock. He pops the wretched mouthpiece into his mouth. We all laugh. Coach, too. It's ten minutes before we can get the wrestle-offs started.

Practice is over. I sit on the shower floor, turning pink under the hottest spray I can endure. We've got the drains plugged with towels and the water is about six inches deep. Visibility is about a foot through the steam. The effect is strange. You hear shouts and splashing, but you seldom see anybody, except when they come up to use your shower and fall over you or when they go sliding by in a seal race.

Two small white legs approach me through the steam. The kneecaps look me in the eye. At this momeent I remember I've left my teeth in the soap dish. I see a blur above me as the small arm reaches. The legs turn and are gone in a splash. The Sausage Man's cackle hangs in the mist.

I'm up and whipping across the cold concrete floor after him, but Sausage is already out the locker room door. Last I see of him he's dancing off across the park, naked, a pink Christmas cherub in black wrestling shoes, cackling and spitting little ice crystals that catch the light from the parking lot and shine like tiny falling stars. He knows if I chase him I'll be late for work.

XI

Here comes Carla in our snow-capped DeSoto. The big old skinny tires squeak and crunch through the dry packed snow. The chrome and snow reflect the street light and for a second or two I'm blind. I'm rubbing my eyes as she pulls up to the curb.

"I have a surprise." She stops. "Are you okay?"

"Fine," I say. "Just blinded for a sec by all the snow."

"The smell of that room probably rotted your eyes," she says as I walk around to the passenger side. The locker room is in shadow. She hasn't noticed I'm toothless.

I nearly sit on the surprise.

"Watch out!" cries Carla.

"Raaahrr!" cries the surprise.

The surprise makes it out of the way, but I do catch Carla's hands, pinning them under my fatigued butt.

"Gotcha," I say, looking fondly down into my lap, bubbling with red curls.

"Hullock," mumbles Carla into the mohair. "You almost squished our new Katzenburger."

94

An emaciated gray and black kitten roams the tops of the front seats. I loft it, give it a couple good rubs along the soft gray flannel headliner, and set it gently down on Carla's head.

"Nice Katzen," Carla gasps affectionately. Mohair upholstery is all kinds of fun in terms of tactile sensation, but it's hell to try to breathe through.

I remove the kitten, scrutinizing it at arm's length. The little critter is indeed undernourished. I check for gender. Her survival seems dubious.

"Katzen B.!" squeals a freed Carla, grabbing the little beast and nuzzling it nose to nose. She hands the kitten back to me and notices that my visage has changed some. "Oh, my God—your teeth!" she exclaims, with a hand tender on my slackened mandible. "Did they break?"

"That bastard-assed dwarf Thuringer stole them," I explain as little Katzenburger crawls inside my coat, curls near my heart, and falls asleep, purring like a diesel, healthier than she appears.

"Why would Damon do something like that?" Carla asks as we crunch off toward the hotel.

"Vendetta," I answer. "Otto and I tied him up and hid him under his blankets. He missed practice. Coach didn't even notice he was gone. If Coach hadn't sat on him by accident when we started our wrestle-offs, Sausage might never have been discovered. We just wanted to temper his hubris a little."

"But you said he has a tough match Tuesday."

"It's not wise to take such things too seriously," I say. "It's only a game."

"Someone should knock hell out of you." Carla smiles.

"Somehow I feel that at this very moment just such an act is being planned." I sink deep into the comfort of our good old car. Katzenburger squeaks. Carla pulls to the curb and examines her, curled in the downy fold of my parka.

"She's not very well," Carla says, pulling back into traffic. "But she's better than when we got her."

"When did we get her?" I ask.

"Dad brought her home this afternoon. He sent someone up to some valley to deliver a car and Katzen was in the car the guy brought back."

Dad's Honda dealership is going fairly strong now. About the only people who buy them are college types, Dad says. But there are six colleges around Spokane, so that should give him enough customers to stay in business until a few more of our countrymen decide they've got better things to do with their money than spend it on gas. Dad sometimes wishes there were a little American car as good as the Honda he could sell. But I tell him to forget it, that he can't afford that kind of economic patriotism. During the season I don't get much time to hang around the store, so I don't know all his salesmen yet. I do know he sent someone up to the Okanogan Valley to deliver a Honda Civic and pick up an Olds. The reason I know this is because the guy was also supposed to pick up a box of apples from Dad's mom. She cooks for the pickers in an apple orchard there. The orchard owners are the ones who bought the Civic. Grandma turned them onto Dad. Apple-picking is long over, of course, but she stays up there anyway. Most of our communication takes the form of boxes of apples. Okanogan Grandma is a little like Columbia River Grandpa. They're separated and they don't like each other much, but they're a lot alike. Grandma won't leave her cabin in the Okanogan, and Grandpa won't leave his cabin on the upper Columbia. Grandma talks to us in apples, and Grandpa speaks in venison steaks.

"The guy told Dad he heard some squeaking in the

back of the car, but he didn't see anything back there. Dad said that when they opened the trunk to see if the spare tire was any good, they found five little kittens. They were very young and very little and four of them were dead. Dad took Katzenburger into his office and put her by the heater and gave her some skim milk. When he brought her home she could hardly walk. We took her to Poodle's doctor, and he gave us some kitten vitamins and said he wouldn't give Katzen her shots for a few weeks and that for only about five weeks old she is a very healthy Katzen. We have to give her vitamins every two hours. Look!"

Carla holds up a plastic dropper bottle filled with a dark bilious substance.

"Smell!" Carla commands.

I smell. My nasal passages are cleared for eternity.

Carla laughs villainously. "Ha!" She bounces up and down on the seat. "Ah ha! We fixed you. That's still not as smelly as your wrestling clothes," she continues gleefully. "But anything worse might be permanently damaging."

"You sure showed me." The stuff doesn't smell that bad, actually. I take a cautious whiff. It just surprises you. "Smells very nutritious," I say, handing it back.

Carla is really happy. I confess without too much self-consciousness that seeing her this way really gets me off. My face expands into a smile. I can't control it. My lips pull back over my gums. Smiling is easier when you don't have any teeth. Probably not as pretty, though.

Carla talks on about the promise of jars and jars of applesauce to be canned and speculates concerning cruelty-to-animals statutes.

I guess I'm a little dizzy. The lights make me a little sick. It's also about 8000 degrees in this car. I crack my window. Carla brings her speculations to a halt.

97

"Don't get too much wind on the Katzen," she warns.

"Just need some air," I respond.

"Louden." She takes my chin in one hand as she guides the DeSoto with the other. "Are you all right?"

"Ah'm hungry," I whimper. "Do you suppose if I called Shute he'd come down to the hotel tonight and wrestle me in one of the banquet rooms? I don't know if I can last another week and a half."

"You could just forget it. You don't have to wrestle him."

"Too late," I say. "I've made my bed. Now I've got to starve and get hell beat out of me in it. I'll eat a little something now; then I'll be okay for work. And maybe you could fix us a snack when I get home. A couple hot fudge sundaes, perhaps? Some rhubarb pie? Two or three double cheeseburgers, maybe?"

"Really?" Carla is wide-eyed.

"No," I sigh.

"How about some applesauce?" Carla suggests.

"Wonderful," I reply. "And I'll pretend it's surrounded by monadnocks of vanilla ice cream."

We turn off Monroe onto Sprague Avenue. Downtown Spokane is all Christmassy. A Lenny Dee version of "Jingle Bell Rock" begins on the hotel's Christmas tape. The organ notes fall in flakes. The black Santa rings his bell, smiling at Carla. I take some deep breaths and feel better.

Carla is talking to me.

"Hmmmm?" I ask.

"Damon—will he give you back your teeth?"

"I imagine," I answer. "They'll be too big for him."

Carla grabs the kitten from inside my coat. She pushes me out the door. I turn back for a good-bye.

"It's sure nice to have a little live thing," she says. Her eyes glow like electric chestnuts.

"It sure is," I reply, getting a peck on the cheek from Carla and a moist little nose rub from the kitten.

At the door I look back. Carla is holding Katzenburger up to the window, waving her little paw. "Wave good-bye to Daddy," she commands.

XII

I keep my mouth closed a lot during work. Sally thinks it's a "damn shame" and Elmo knows where I can get a set of red, white, and blue enamels made. I'm considering the idea. I could base my practice on being the doctor with the patriotic smile.

The phone starts ringing with dinner orders and I begin to feel my self-discipline slip away. I put down three wheat-germ burgers before pulling myself together.

"Lemon Pie is still here," Sally says, handing me 611's order. I wonder what the guy does with all his lemon pie.

He's naked again. Not even a towel, the brazen fucker. He's got what my grandfather calls a soft-off. His cock flaps limp as a whitefish. They're everywhere in the Columbia now that it doesn't flow any more. I used to sit for hours in front of Grandpa's cabin pulling them in. The ones I didn't fling at rattlesnakes I'd stuff into a gunnybag. I'd get a bagful and we'd bury them in Grandpa's corn patch.

The guy asks about my teeth, so I tell him about Thuringer. He asks how I lost them originally and I tell him about the incredible monster from Issaquah who ran my face into a corner of the bleachers in the state tournament my sophomore year. It knocked a bunch of my teeth out and broke my nose. I think he was the only guy I ever wrestled that I actually got mad at. He'd been state champ the year before and was pissed I was beating him.

"I didn't realize you were still in school," the guy says, pulling some photographs from his attaché case.

I admit to a certain curiosity concerning them. He spreads his pictures across the bed. One draws me. It's of a well-built-gone-to-fat guy with the giantest cock I've ever seen. It looks like a loaf of French bread. The glans penis is about half as round as the faces of the four pubescent boys who lap wondrously at it. I'm reminded of one of Otto's road-trip boy scout reminiscences: "Shit," Otto said. "It's just like sucking on your finger."

The guy says he's leaving tomorrow, but that he'll be back in a couple weeks. He's sorry we can't get together. He has a guest coming. He'll leave the tray in the hall.

I consider listening at the door when I make my pickup rounds.

Downstairs, Sally informs me that she's heard Lemon Pie is a queer. She's checked the register and his name is . . . I tune her out. It's none of my business. Tuning her back in, I hear he's from Walla Walla. Somehow it's good to know that homosexuals come from someplace besides San Francisco. I decide not to listen at the door. In fact, the morning crew can get his tray.

I'm feeling pretty good, generally. I take all stairs two at a time. I loft the heaviest trays of dirty dishes to my

shoulder, balancing them on my fingertips, flexing my fingers frequently, exercising those unsung muscles of a good grip, the interossei and lumbricales. I reflect upon the tracks a good grip will leave on wrists and upper arms. Dishes brush my ear. Turkey gravy, bits of dressing, peaks of burned meringue deck my hair. Each time I see Sally for a new order she picks the garbage off my head.

Elmo and I arm wrestle. I beat him both arms. I bounce on my toes while Elmo runs the charcoal brick over his grill. His tools are cleaned and put away in their slots in the cutting board. It's about time to head home.

I've never been more in touch with my body than I am at this weight. I swear I can hear the valves of my heart open and slam shut. Oxygenated blood swooshes through my arteries. It sounds like the Seattle Monorail. Leukocytes and erythrocytes politely line up at my capillaries: "Be my guest!" "No, no. After you!" they say.

My highly energized state strikes Elmo as comical. Wiping the grill a final few times with his burlap rag, he looks up at me and smiles. "You get you some teeth, you be a totally tuned man," he says, chuckling. "You about a yard off the floor. Best be sure you come down on that Shute."

I smile and dance and hold my palms up for him to punch. He throws a combination, blowing out his nose each time his fist smacks my palm. The veins bulge beneath the tatoos on Elmo's forearms. He was a lightweight fighter in Chicago in the 1940s. He's the only black adult I've ever known, besides teachers and coaches. I'm sure glad he got out of boxing with his brain intact.

Sally looks up from balancing her till. She's already pulled the velvet cord across the doorway. It's been a pretty slow night in the dining room.

"Merry Christmas, Elmo," I say, shaking his hand. I'm off for the next week and a half. I arranged it way back when I decided I'd wrestle Shute.

"Merry Christmas to you," Elmo says.

I give Sally a peck. "Merry Christmas, Sal!"

"Good luck, Louden," Sally says.

XIII

The asphalt alleys are glazed with ice and shine like new black nylon wrestling shoes. I fall on my ass occasionally. The snow melted from the heat of all the stores and signs and people and cars downtown, but now after the stores are closed it's freezing again. Riverside and Monroe are both still slushy, though, because of all the kids cruising. But the alleys I run are iced up.

Crossing the Monroe Street bridge is a pain. Creeps of all sorts honk and leer and fling ice balls at me. I recognize some David Thompson kids, so I wave. As I run along I wonder where Shute might be now. I *know* where Shute is: he's out running up some mountain through heavy snow, ready to pound Christmas out of Santa Claus.

I feel good when I cross the bridge. Now I can run down side streets. I crunch crisply through the snowy streets. Peripherally, I see the little chunks of snow flying from my boots. Everywhere the night is brightened by the clean snow. Under the street lights it sparkles. Colored Christmas lights are a muted glow beneath the snow in hedges and firs. They remind me of Harmoniums—happy glowing little creatures living within the planet Mercury in a Kurt Vonnegut book, *The Sirens of Titan*. I feel good. The air tastes good. I roll my arms in wide circles from the shoulders and watch the running angel shadow. But there are two. Running footsteps crunch behind me. I stop and turn. Bundled and panting, cap hanging elflike, the Sausage Man stands in a cloud of vapor. He hands me something. It's a frozen plastic bag. I gape.

"Your teeth," Sausage says. "I'm sorry they froze. I put them in some water like my grandfather does and they froze solid."

Sure enough, there's my partial plate embedded in a block of ice.

"Thanks, Sausage," I say. "Hope you didn't get cold or in trouble or anything running out of the locker room that way."

"No sweat," says the Sausage Man, starting to jog. "The Russian hockey team does that shit all the time."

"How was your run?" Carla asks from the bottom of the basement stairs.

"Okay," I say. "Sausage caught me down by the bridge and gave me back my teeth." I hold up the plastic bag.

"Frozen shrimp?" Carla guesses.

"Teeth," I reply. "He put them in water and they froze. He ran with me up to the park and we met Kuch and ran three through the snow on the track. I hope Mash doesn't do him permanent harm."

I'm beat by this time. I take the stairs one at a time, clinging to the rail with one hand and to my boots and rucksack and sweats and teeth with the other. My T-shirt sticks so tight it's epidermal. Sweat drips from my jock and dots the tile.

"Look!" Carla points to the kitten. It's snuggled up to a little teddy bear I won for Carla arm wrestling at the Whitworth College carnival. And it's nursing, sucking loudly at the fur on the bear's foot.

"It's nursing!" I exclaim with tired astonishment.

"A surrogate mother," Carla informs me as the kitten slurps away in contented ignorance.

Seems to me like pretty aberrant behavior. But "wow" is all I have energy enough to say on the subject for now.

"The DeSoto looks beautiful!" I yell from the shower. The old blue and gray couldn't have looked better when it was new over thirty years ago.

"Katzen helped me!"

I relax against the shower wall, devouring the applesauce that was waiting for me on the scales. It's cold and good and the water is hot and good. I weigh 148. My teeth are beginning to emerge from the block of ice in the soap dish. I'm glad to be out of school and off work for a while. I try like hell to fill my life with things to do, but sometimes they get to be too much. I smile at Carla's name for the kitten. To Carla every cat is "Katzen" and every dog is "Doggels-Doggels." She named the teddy bear "Bilbo."

Carla's in bed. She's pillowed up against the headboard, looking awfully comfortable and cozy in her floppy flannel nightgown, reading a little booklet entitled *Your New Kitten*. Naked, I bend my knees for the vault into bed.

"Eeeeeh!" Carla gives a little scream, tempered by her consideration for Dad sleeping above us. "The Katzen!" she says, lifting kitten and bear from my intended ground zero and placing them at the foot of the bed.

106

I settle in. Carla turns off the light. We cuddle.

"We're going to have a guest for breakfast," Carla whispers, pointing to the ceiling.

"Is she decent?" I ask.

"I didn't see her. Katzen and I were waxing," she replies.

"Thanks for the applesauce," I say. "It was good."

"You're welcome," Carla says.

I tug clumsily at Carla's nightgown. She pulls it off and flings it. The kitten squeaks. I always get a rush at the sight of Carla naked, even when it's dark and I can't really see her. I tremble.

We make slow love, lying on our sides, tummy to tummy, like old people probably do.

We touch and kiss lightly, practicing our tenderness. I hold her bottom so she doesn't fall away. It's just a handful.

Once, when we'd only made love a few times, just after I'd come Carla asked me what I was thinking. I didn't want to lie, so I said I was thinking of the salmon on the Columbia when it was a river and how they'd leap the falls to swim upstream. She didn't say anything. One of the next times we made love, by some miracle we came together. Recovering, we looked into each other's eyes. "There they go," Carla said, smiling. At first I didn't get it—salmon and the Columbia were far from my mind. But in a second or two I did, and smiled back. "There they go," I said. The phrase has since become ritual when our love is at its best.

Half lost in reverie of the loves we've made and the love we're making and just too tired to control myself, I come too soon.

"I'm sorry," I breathe.

Carla's hands pace softly the back of my neck. "There they go," she sighs.

XIV

We had a guest for breakfast, all right. And for the rest of Saturday and Christmas Eve and Christmas Day.

And she is decent. I put her to the test right away, sprinting upstairs in my boxer shorts and whipping off a hundred quick pushups on the kitchen floor as she scrambled eggs.

"You must be Louden," she said, unperturbed.

"I'm Carla," I replied. "Louden's a lot prettier and can do pushups to infinity."

"My name is Cindy," she said. She's built like a middle-distance runner. She says she skies a little, but I bet she skies a lot. She's tan as a football. And she sure seems awful young for Dad.

"Howdy, Cindy," I said, puffing a bit somewhere in the nineties. I was bearing down hard on one hundred when she turned from the stove and hooked my arm with her foot. I fell square on my nose.

"Oh, I'm so sorry," said Cindy, gathering plates from the cupboard. She was definitely insincere.

I laughed, figuring it a good move and a greeting commensurate with mine. I whipped off my last pushups as the blood dripped slow and steady.

Turning, Cindy saw the blood. "Bloody nose?" she inquired.

"Soaking up through the floor from the laundry room," I replied. "I beat hell out of Dad's girl friends and stash 'em down there. They make quite a pile."

"I bet they do. How might one avoid such a fate?" she asked, dropping a paper towel to the floor.

"Can't be sure," I said, wiping my nose and then the floor.

"Perhaps time will tell."

"I imagine so. It tells everything else."

"Larry tells me you won't be joining us for breakfast," Cindy said, beginning to set the table. Larry is my dad. Lawrence Swain. No middle initial.

"Dazz right, Honey! Dazzz right!" I was imitating Elmo, smiling big and bright. "I don't eat no regula' foods. I just eats a few old raza blades and chews da concrete ofen da basement walls."

"I hope the house doesn't fall down!" she yelled after me.

"Me, too!" I yelled over my shoulder from the stairs.

I had to stuff some toilet paper in my nose and get dressed. Coach gave me a bunch of little gauze nose stoppers, but I'm all out. My nose has been cauterized twice. That seals the vessels for a while, but as the nose continues to get whacked with forearms and be ground into wrestling mats, the vessels break again in new places. Blood runs so close to the surface of the inside of my nose a rapid rise in temperature can turn it loose.

Carla was tired from waxing the DeSoto, so I let her sleep till time for work. Besides babysitting, she still sells health foods on weekends at the New Pioneer and she's going to work full time over the Christmas vacation. Little Katzenburger idled steadily from her nest in Carla's nightgown at the foot of the bed.

Carla likes it that Cindy's hair is soft and not lacquered and stacked like spun glass. Women beyond twenty-five have this tendency to look like Christmas decorations. I see them all the time at the hotel, looking like they had their hair done in the bakery.

At first Carla was a little dubious about Cindy leaving her little girl with her grandparents. She thought it might not be too wise of Cindy at such an important time for kids as Christmas. I thought the kid maybe suffered from some hideous deformity or childhood disease. Carla called me a maniac and punched me hard in the stomach when I told her that.

Cindy spoiled our speculations, however, by bringing the kid over on Christmas Eve to open presents with us. Her name is Willa. The little creature looked okay to me. A pain in the ass, as most toddler types are—giggly and drooly and sporadically weepy—but healthy enough. We kept Katzenburger downstairs. Kids can get pretty physical with baby animals, and we want Katzen to develop strength and sharpen her instincts for survival before we let her out in the world. Besides, she's about half stuck to that bear.

After Cindy brought Willa over, Carla began to think Cindy's leaving her with her grandparents had just been a courteous gesture in case we might not dig little kids, and probably part of a plan to go slow and easy on Dad.

It certainly was courteous. I can stand about fifteen seconds of those cookie-crumbling rug rats. But Carla enjoyed it. She took Willa down to see "the baby katzen." She showed her how to get her doll to talk and helped her warm its bottle. She bundled her up and took her out to play in the snow awhile, then pulled her on a short sled ride. I watched them out the window.

It wasn't that bad a time. Carla helped her make a little bed out of the wrapping paper and one of my new flannel shirts and Willa went to sleep in it under the Christmas tree.

Cindy talked some about skiing and her job with an ad agency and about the movies and books she likes. She likes *Jesus Christ Superstar,* too, but she said she couldn't understand why I'd seen it eleven times, especially since I'm not even a believer. I told her it was food for my soul.

"Your soul?" she said.

"It can't live on the promise of milk and honey alone," I said and gave her a hungry-cherub grin as my stomach growled mightily, interrupting *Miracle on 34th Street,* which we'd been half watching.

"That's not your soul," Cindy said, smiling.

The ad agency Cindy works for has done business with Dad for a long time. I remembered that the name on the inside covers of those books on Dad's nightstand is C. Callus—Cindy. And I wondered how long Dad'd been seeing her.

And then as we sat in the soft candlelight with the snow shining in through the window and the Christmas-tree smell fresh in the air and a miracle having only shortly transpired on TV, I got to thinking about Mom and being lonesome for her and wondering what new dishes she got herself for Christmas. But later, just as I was about to call her, she called me. And though she said she missed me, she sounded real happy, too. Her stepkids were yelling and screaming and having a good time in the background. I thanked her for the heavy-duty suspenders and she thanked me for the new tapes for her fat-assed Buick.

It continues to amaze me that Carla doesn't get homesick for her parents. She contends they're assholes, and they must be if she doesn't miss them at Christmas. Maybe she's just made up her mind not to.

I let my spirits get a little low on the way up to the park to meet Kuch and run our three. I guess I haven't really gotten over feeling a little weird about Mom and Dad. Stupid as it is, I kind of wish marriages would last forever. Actually, I sometimes wish everything would last forever. This is a wish I fight hard but am not always able to defeat. Really, I'm proud of Mom and Dad for having the strength to fight for big-time happiness after twenty years of something that must not have been enough. Christ, it must take guts to break up at the age of fifty, then go right out and find somebody new to love better. I get about half choked up just throwing away my sweat clothes at the end of the season. I've poured out so much of my life in them. I'd probably save them if they weren't so smelly and disintegrated.

The end of the year is just a bad time for me anyway. I get to thinking about Time moving and I have to fight hard not to be depressed. In a few years, no matter how healthy I am, my brain cells will begin to die. I could be the most heavy-duty stud in the northern hemisphere, the ace exobiologist or space physicist in the world, and I'd still really be nothing but a candidate for motehood in the sweep of Time's great dustcloth. If Time can take the Columbia River and turn it into a big fucking lake, there's no limit to what it can do to me.

My entire relationship with the world changes when I allow myself to get that low. I could actually feel the night go dull around me. I could feel strength leave my muscle tissue. I was beginning to feel the cold. The sparkle of the stars and the glow of the snow, the sharpness of my footsteps and the steady songs of my body—my pulse and my breathing—were pulling away from me. I knew I'd lose them for sure if my spirit couldn't close the ground. I'd just been jogging, so I started to run. I kicked my knees up high and blew my breath out in sharp whacks against the cold. I spat into the shadows and sent my physical and spiritual warriors on the warpath.

I felt a lot better when I hit the park. The night was sharp again and my blood was rumbling. I had a strong buffer stoked up against the cold. Christmas carols wafted faintly from the Lutheran church. They have a tape that runs day and night. They play it real low and it creates a fairyland atmosphere. What can it hurt? I half expected to see Jesus crunching moodily through the park. Poor fucker with all those wasted dreams, all those deluded souls on his back. For a second I thought I did see him off across the track. But it was only Kuch, sneaking from tree to tree, fixing to surprise-attack me.

We gave Dad the word on Cindy this morning at breakfast. "A decent woman," I said. "A good person," Carla said. We left it at that, not wanting to overbear.

XV

To get to see the deer you take Indian Trail Road past the dump almost to Indian Painted Rocks, then turn off on a road the county keeps plowed so they can drive out and dump pelleted alfalfa for the deer. Unless you drive some kind of snow vehicle or a car like our 1941 DeSoto, it's fairly easy to get stuck, even with the road plowed. The DeSoto is heavy as a mastodon, and with sixteen-inch wheels and a fluid-drive transmission, we cannot get stuck on level ground. Providing the snow isn't unreasonably deep, that is. Just in case, I've got the trunk loaded with sand bags.

We brought our tape player and some appropriate deer-watching tapes, a few cold steamed vegetables, a thermos of tea with honey, a can of chicken-vegetable baby food for Katzen, and her blanket and her bear and her vitamins and pooping pan. We had a full tank of gas so we could keep the motor running and the heater going all night, and Dad and I triple-checked the exhaust system for leaks. Some snowshoed and industrious ax murderer might have gotten us, but carbon monoxide didn't have a prayer. We wore our longies and our parkas and brought along two down sleeping bags and our pillows. We pulled up about thirty yards from a salt lick and turned off the head lights. We left the dash lights on low for the soft green glow they have.

It was plenty dark, but still early evening. There weren't any deer around yet, so Carla figured it would be a good time to get out and put Katzen's dinner to warming on the exhaust manifold. Way back last summer when Carla and I took our first camping trip together, about a half hour from the campground I pulled the pickup off the road and wired a can of beef stew to the exhaust manifold. After we pitched our tent we had hot stew ready for us without starting a fire or pumping a stove. Carla got sold on the idea and now keeps a can of hash or stew or meatballs and gravy in the trunk in case of emergency hunger, which is the only kind of hunger under which, she says, such canned crap should be consumed.

I learned cooking on the manifold from the cat skinners on the Trapper Peak fire. I spent two weeks on the fire line during the summer of my sophomore year, just before I found work at the hotel. Every day about an hour before lunch the manifolds of the big cats would be ringed with cans. From a distance they looked like Hawaiian leis strung around the big diesel engines. And it looked like a rowdy luau when a can would explode because somebody forgot to punch a hole in it so the heat could get out.

I could only take two weeks of fire fighting. The money was great and the work was fun and exciting and good for me, but the life up there was just too dirty and uncomfortable. I may look like one rough country sonofabitch, but inside I'm all wall-to-wall carpet and big soft chairs. It could also get dangerous. A few days after I got home I heard on the news that a couple guys got killed up there. The fire started to run and a ranger went to see if anybody was left in its way. He must have misjudged the fire's speed, because it got around him and cut him off. One of the dozer drivers got to the ranger, but the fire was burning so hard by then they couldn't get out. So the dozer driver scooped out a hole and drove the cat over it, and he and the ranger crawled in. When the fire burned past and people could get to them, they found them without a burn on their bodies. They had suffocated because the fire burned all their air.

Carla putting the baby food on the manifold reminded me of Trapper Peak. You'd lie in camp in your paper sleeping bag that the Forest Service gives you, with ashes and soot and fire retardant in your hair, just wishing you could get a hot shower somewhere. And you'd be looking off at the little burning spots on the hill when all of a sudden a tree would just explode. The fire would be burning in the humus and roots, and when the trees reached their kindling temperature they'd go up in a big swoosh and a flame a couple hundred feet high. The sky would get like dawn for a few seconds, then go black again.

Katzen had taken her vitamins, eaten some chicken and veggies, and shit way out of her league in terms of both volume and stench before the first deer appeared. We were parked near some trees where the feed and salt are protected from heavy snow. The deer come down from the mountains and across an open field to get their dinner. I was out cleaning Katzen's pan when I saw five or six whitetails strung out across the field. Carla had to open a window because of Katzen's bad smell and so an odor of kitty shit and strains of Johann Pachelbel floated from the car into the night. The deer weren't sure what was going down at their favorite nightspot. The owls and night hawks had been replaced by a more classical, less hygienic group.

When I got back in, Carla had things straightened around. Katzen was in the front seat nested in her blanket, sucking away at the leg of her bear. I set her pooping pan on the floor in front of her. In back Carla had set the plastic box of veggies and the tape player on the rear window deck and spread one sleeping bag over the back seat. The other bag was partly over her and partly left for me. I took off my boots and set them on the floor next to Carla's and climbed carefully over the high old front seat.

"Here they come," I said as Carla handed me a cup of steamy tea. The good smell of the tea and honey was driving out the smell of Katzen's foul and precocious clinker. I stuck my nose almost in the tea and inhaled the rich soft fragrance. I licked the tea dew off my mustache and pointed so Carla could see the deer. She had to twist around to get a good view, so we changed places. We grunted and tugged and stretched and tunneled and held cups of tea carefully. We fluffed pillows and re-tucked each other a little and snuggled our feet. When we were all comfortable and ready to watch deer, Carla looked out the window and smiled and her eyes got big because the deer had come up to the feed while we were rearranging ourselves and stood around the car, none of them more than twenty yards away. We could hear them chewing.

I believe in preparing for things. Even little things like seeing the deer can be more fun if you cut down the number of potentially unpleasant variables. For example, we had a full tank of gas and a good heater and a perfect exhaust system. We had lots of warm clothes and warm and comfortable coverings and some good stuff to

117

eat and drink. We had music we liked, and some baby food and a reliable bear to pacify Katzen if she got colicky or whatever baby animals get that might make them raise a racket. We had the trunk filled with sand bags to keep us from getting stuck, but just in case I'd brought along a couple shovels. And I had a few flares.

Carla goes along with this, especially the music and vegetables, but she is only lukewarm about my last variable limiter, the .9mm Luger that I stow under the seat and sleep with on almost all camping trips. I admit I am not completely sold on the idea of having a gun along, but I am committed to it for now because I just believe our lives are too important to leave even relatively unprotected. I mean, I'm pretty strong and probably fairly up to fighting for our lives, but I can't punch out a bullet or turn knife steel to rubber. Also, there are guys around who could beat me to death in a very few minutes with nothing but their fists and feet. I mean, we're vulnerable enough just in relation to things like disease and bad moods, without leaving ourselves open to attacks by other human beings. Animals don't worry me.

The problem, of course—and this is another variable —is that someone trying to hurt us might get to the gun first. I mean there are some arch motherfucking weirdos running around—even in the Northwest. Last summer, a social worker in a Triumph Spitfire picked up two hitchhikers near Missoula, and they killed him and cut off his fingers and ears for jewelry and ate his heart. This fall, some poor crazy asshole strapped a dozen sticks of dynamite around his middle and walked into the schoolhouse up on the reservation and hugged his estranged wife, who was substitute teaching, and blew the whole fucking place into the happy hunting ground. And that was three or four miles from our cabin on Loon Lake. But you can't let stuff like that worry you into a preoccupation. It would diminish all the neat stuff about being alive. I just try to forget about it but still be ready.

I really didn't make a very active deer watcher last night. I've seen plenty of deer and I was pretty sleepy, so I didn't pay as much attention as Carla. I mostly just wanted to relax. I was dancing my toes to a quiet Don McLean tune called "Winterwood" when Carla said softly, "Here come some more."

Sure enough, four more deer stood at the edge of the trees.

"Are those mule deer?" Carla asked.

"I can't tell," I said. "I'd have to see their tails." You're supposed to be able to tell mule deer by their big ears, but I never can. They're also supposed to be stockier than whitetails.

"I think they're mule deer," Carla said.

I sat with my eyes closed, very comfortably tucked in my corner of the DeSoto, wondering why you see more falling stars in summer than in winter. I opened my eyes and looked at Carla and then closed them again and stretched my leg until my foot found her thermal crotch. Her hand rubbed across my big wool boot sock and patted my foot. Then I felt some woolly toes pad along my inner thigh and then a warm squirrelly foot tried to make off with my acorns before I trapped it. Feeling each other's pressure was all we were after.

"They are mule deer," Carla whispered. "They have very big ears compared to the others." And her toes gave me a prod that said, "I told you so." It also made me instantly horny.

Carla felt it with her foot and responded with more pressure. To which my cock responded with increased turgidity. "You're supposed to relax for tomorrow," she said.

"I think it would be very relaxing," I replied.

"And don't forget," Carla said on her way over to my side of the seat, "you said it burns up two hundred calories."

"We have a secret from these deer," was the last thing I remember hearing before Carla woke me in the garage this morning. She said I was sleeping so soundly when we got home from seeing the deer that she didn't want to wake me to come down to bed.

XVI

I decided to walk home from Dr. Livengood's office. I weigh 149 1/2 on his scale, so I need all the exercise I can get. It turned out that getting his permission to drop the weight was no sweat at all. He just listened to my story, then to my chest, then pushed me on the scale. He read off 50, but it was really 49 1/2.

"Shouldn't be any problem. A little jogging and a healthy shit ought to do it now," he said, and smiled. "Flush out that Christmas turkey."

"Wouldn't have seemed like Christmas without a little white meat and turkey gravy." I smiled sheepishly. I nearly lost control at the dinner table yesterday.

Dr. Livengood smiled again and patted me on the shoulder as though I were a little kid and then took my weight-loss form over to his desk and signed it. Over his shoulder he handed me a Christmas card. It was from Max Mokeskey, the med student who had done his preceptorship here. Max sent his greetings to Dr. and Mrs. Livengood and in a P.S. said, "Please give Louden Swain my wishes for good luck in his big wrestling match."

"Gee," I said. "That's really nice of him to remember me."

"He's a good boy," Dr. Livengood said, handing me back my weight-loss form.

"Boy," Dr. Livengood called him. Max is probably twenty-seven or twenty-eight years old. He stands probably six-four and goes maybe 220. "Boy." I really get a bang out of old people.

God, it's a beautiful day! Carla drove to work early just to drop me off at Dr. Livengood's. It's still pretty early. My appointment was for eight and it only took about ten minutes. People are still on their way to work. Carla's probably drinking tea with Belle right now, sitting on a granola barrel, waiting for nine o'clock and the first customers.

We got just enough snow last night to cover up the dog shit on the sidewalks and the bus exhaust spores in the streets. Ordinarily I'd avoid a busy street like Monroe on a walk from town. But now the traffic is slow and soft-sounding. The cars and buses seem like a herd of big, friendly animals headed for grazing ground. All of us emit little clouds of vapor. I imagine us as comic book characters with writing in our clouds. A snow-capped Toyota pickup has turned into a pronghorn antelope. Dressed in a camp cook's apron and hat, it waves a ladle and hails me in Kuch's voice.

"Howdy, pilgrim," says the antelope-cook. "How's about warmin' up yur ribs with a little wild onion stew?"

"No thanks, ole stud hoss," I say. "Can't even take time to set. Headed for the winter rendezvous up to Fort David Thompson. Figure to wrestle Gary Shute out of all his hides and his poke o' gold."

"That Shute's quick as a snake an' mean as an old

mountain lion," yells the pronghorn from far down the trail. "Best watch yur topknot!"

"Best watch yourn!" I yell back. But the little cook is gone, the chuckwagon obscured by the lumbering buffalo buses. Yesterday afternoon just before Christmas dinner I finished reading a book called *Mountain Man* by Vardis Fisher. I'm really a sucker for a good wilderness story. Kuch had been after me to read that book for a long time.

I like feeling a kinship with traffic. I like pretending. Carla would get a kick out of seeing me this way.

She really loved seeing the deer last night. I had a great night, too, even though Christmas night has traditionally been an anticlimax for me. But Christmas Eve is a gas all day. I always go to a matinee, then open presents at night and have a great time at home. But Christmas night is always a bummer, because everything I've looked forward to is over. This Christmas night was different because of Carla and the deer, and because the thing I've been looking forward to most isn't Christmas presents—it's my match with Shute. Also, I'm just growing up.

Carla and Cindy made yogurt all afternoon, Kuch and his dad were somewhere racing snowmobiles, and Otto hates *Jesus Christ Superstar,* so I went to the matinee alone. I half wanted to go alone anyway, but I called Kuch and Otto because since we were in grade school we've always gone to a matinee on Christmas Eve.

Nobody except Carla understands why I like *Jesus Christ Superstar* so much. And even though she understands, she can't get into it herself. I guess my reasons are pretty personal and fairly dumb. It's just that I've always wanted to believe that story, and this movie version concentrates on some believable aspects.

Christ is a guy who has committed himself to a goal

none of his people clearly understands. He is disciplined and calculating in pursuit of the goal. He defines his whole reality as though the goal—eternal life for himself and everybody who believes in him—were really possible. He lives fierce and proud and then he dies. In the movie he is resurrected, but it's okay because you feel like he deserves it. I don't for a second believe Christ or anybody else lives on eternally, except maybe for a while as a memory or an artifact. But I do think a lot of people deserve to. I think old Jay Gatz in *The Great Gatsby* would certainly deserve to if he were a real person, and I think my mom and dad do. But that's not the only reason I'm hooked on J.C.

I *know* the characters in that movie. They're real. In all my younger days in Sunday school I never heard one biblical story about characters I figured I knew. I didn't even believe the living people in Mom's church were real. But in the movie everybody yells and fights and cries and sweats and farts and probably fucks, and Judas has some noble qualities, and Simon is an archfreak and dancin' fool who slobbers like the Sausage Man, and Jesus warns God he'd best take him soon before he changes his mind, and that poor fucking Pilate just wants to let Jesus off, but he can't because it's not part of the way things are defined.

Pilate is a figure who really interests me. After I had seen J.C. a few times I ran across this book called *The Master and Margarita* at a garage sale. The cover implies it's about the devil and supernatural stuff and I bought it for that interest. It is about the devil, but it turns out to be about a lot more, too. It's mostly a satire on Russian artists' unions, I guess. Anyway, Pilate is a character in it. Bulgakov, the author, shows Pilate suffering in the immortality he achieved through his part in Christ's superstardom.

I can't figure out whether God meant Pilate's immortality as a reward or a punishment. He must have meant it as a reward, or at least a compensation, because Pilate sure couldn't be blamed for Jesus's death. Pilate didn't have any choice. He couldn't have let Christ off. He got sucked in. He had to stay within the divine scope of events. If he'd let Jesus off, it would have spoiled everything. Pilate was duped. And so was Judas.

Anyway, in *The Master and Margarita*, Pilate and his dog sit on this asteroid way out in space and Pilate wonders and wonders where he went wrong with that crazy Galilean. It's beautiful the way Bulgakov frees Pilate from the asteroid so he and his dog can at least stretch their legs in eternity.

And then aside from what the movie makes me think about, there's what it makes me see and hear and feel. Everybody who had anything to do with the making of that film must be a genius. The singing and dancing and rock and roll are so wild and beautiful. It makes me weak —it truly does—that human folks can produce such sounds and movements.

There are certain points in the movie—like when Jesus is yelling at God about why he has to die—that set me free from my normal consciousness, that disrupt my competitive relationship with life. I mean when Jesus lets blast at God with that shrieking falsetto of his, I get shudders and my eyes tear. I want to jump up and scream some primal sound. What I feel is that I'm a human being and one of my human being teammates has just done a wonderful, beautiful, transcendent fucking thing with our limited human ability. And I'm proud.

It's exactly the same feeling I had at a pep assembly last year when Otto was named Prep Lineman of the Year in Washington. I cried. I'm not ashamed, but I am glad I was sitting in the back row so I could turn my head.

And I had it last summer at the motorcycle races down at Castle Rock. Kuch was leading the novice main until the last lap, when he highsided into the wall coming out of the last corner. His dad and I went running out there after the pack went by to see how he was. He was going sixty or seventy when he crashed, and I figured he at least broke his back. But when we got to the corner he had his helmet off and was just leaning back against the wall, shaking his head slowly and looking at the sky. When his dad saw Kuch was okay he slowed down and we walked across the track to where Kuch and the bike were. Mr. Kuchera knelt and said, "Kenny, you've got to turn the gas down sometime." They were so beautiful at that moment it made me feel like I was pretty neat just because I was their friend.

And then I had it again this fall watching *Wide World of Sports*. Pelé was playing his last soccer game. I don't know anything about Pelé except what everybody else knows—that along with Muhammad Ali, Pelé is one of the world's best-known human beings and greatest athletes. He's supposed to be from humble beginnings and all that. I probably wouldn't even have watched the program if it hadn't come on right after football and if Balldozer, whose stepmother is Brazilian, hadn't threatened to kill me if I switched the channel.

So about a quarter into the game—right in the middle of the action—Pelé whips off his jersey and starts to jog around the stadium. All the players stop and the crowd wails and freaks out. The camera came up close on Pelé, and he was waving his jersey high and flashing his ivories wide and crying like a baby. Then they switched to the actual sound inside the stadium, and unless you understood Portuguese you couldn't hear a thing but foreign and semi-insane screaming. They had a guy trying to translate, but you couldn't hear him. It didn't matter to me, anyway, because all I could think about was Pelé's face. And my eyes filled up with tears for him and all his great days of playing. I wish every human being in the world sometime in his life could know the glory of tears like Pelé's. And I hope I can, too.

I walked home from the movie happy as a fish and about two feet off the ground, just psyched about being alive and aware of all the possibilities. I stayed about that high through the evening and finally came down on the way to the park when I began thinking about Mom and Dad and another year going by and all the possibilities. A person sure doesn't have to be a great athlete or politician or doctor or artist or entrepreneur or performer of any type or degree of greatness to find challenge in life. About half the time I think it's a great victory just to be able to smile semiregularly, to keep your head up, to keep from giving in and getting mean. I'm not ashamed to admit I need regular transfusions of confidence to keep me going. I need some examples that remind me, by God, it can be done.

When I got home from the park I polished all Dad's shoes and oiled Carla's boots even though they didn't really need it. I didn't think I was sleepy, but I figured I should go to bed because I didn't want to be tired the next night and fall asleep in the middle of seeing the deer. But as soon as I cuddled up to Carla's back and got myself all contoured and warmed, I fell right to sleep and slept like an old tree till morning.

XVII

The phone rings me out of my reverie. It's junior high and Otto and I are in Belle's basement watching her big brother and his friends take turns violating her body. She loves it. They invite us to join in, but we're too embarrassed and scared her mom will come home. We leave and run over to Otto's and flog our dummies raw.

I have a superturgid boner and it hurts to sprint upstairs. I catch the phone on about the zillionth ring. It's Dad waking me for the match. I like to take naps before a match if I can. For some reason they can be absolutely subterranean, so I like to make sure someone wakes me. No doubt I'm riddled with subconscious fears.

Dad wishes me good luck and asks again if I want him to come to the match. I tell him no, that this one won't be much to see, but to be sure to take off early next Tuesday night for the Shute match. He says he won't forget.

Back downstairs the bed's all warm still. Belle was probably the world's most beautiful and licentiously precocious seventh-grader. She really doesn't look much older now, except that the rest of her body has filled out to match her tits. Her legs are like the legs of a race horse, long, smooth-muscled, and precisely defined. In seventh grade she was mostly legs and tits and long pigtails.

I find it strange that even though I could not ask for more or better sex, I still fantasize about other girls. Even sometimes when Carla and I are making love I'll think of Belle. I'll think of coming on her tits, which her brother and his friends did to her great delight. She'd rub it all over with her hands—like suntan lotion. Once when we were making love, I imagined Mrs. Brockington, my history teacher, fucking a horse. I think it was because she had shown us a movie about the potentially future-shocking effects of artificial insemination, or maybe that was the time Tanneran told us about the death of Catherine the Great.

There's almost nothing sexually imaginable Carla is not up for. I guess we could shit on each other or something like that, but we don't. So I don't figure I'm sexually frustrated. I guess maybe I just have a lot of energy that works itself out through my cock.

I think of Belle's nipples all pumped up and brown, of Mrs. Brockington bending over her desk with a horse mounted behind, of Romaine Lewis about to introduce his cock to Carla's lips, of Lemon Pie's pictures of the dick-licking little boys, of Mom. Weird.

It's amazing how fast I come once the images start flashing and how all I can think of now is a hot chocolate float after the match if my weight is down enough.

XVIII

Our junior varsity is down, 19–11. I watch out the wrestling room window as Doug Bowden, our number-two man at fifty-four, shakes hands with some guy I don't know from Lewis and Clark. I assume Doug will put this guy away in short order. Doug would be number one on a lot of other teams, but the two of us have been in the same weight class these past two and a half years now and I've beaten him steady. We both lettered as sophomores because the senior I beat out for number one quit. That left a guy named Warren Morford, who should have wrestled at forty-five but didn't want to lose the weight. Warren was heavy into anchovy pizzas, and Kuch would treat him to one every chance he got so Warren wouldn't get to thinking about dropping down to forty-five, where Kuch was number one after Lynn Atkinson broke his neck sledding. Doug and Warren had some real battles. Whoever won would be so beat when it came time to wrestle me that I wasn't getting enough workout, which was Coach's motivation for the tough preparation drill we use now. If a guy's not being pushed enough, or if he has an especially tough match, Coach will run him thirty-second rounds against the number-one men in the weight classes above. All next week, for example, I'll be wrestling Smith and Balldozer and Otto, one after the other, every thirty seconds, just as fast as we can go. I'm going to ask Coach to put Kuch in when I'm really tired so I'll have somebody lighter and faster—somebody like Shute—to work against.

"Lunch time!" I yell down to the mats below. "Lunch time, Dougie. Eat 'im, eat 'im, eat 'im!" Carla contends we wrestlers are all a bunch of suppressed puff-jobbers with our continual references to oral relations.

"Burn 'im, Dougie! Sting 'im! Take it to 'im one time!" yells Randy Smith, Doug's best friend, from the other side of the window.

The bleachers are about full and most of the cheerleaders are here. The junior varsity matches usually start with a small crowd, just parents of the wrestlers and the few really interested people who want good seats for the varsity match. But by the time they get to the 154-pound class the gym is usually about full and the crowd is into it.

Belle stomps her feet and claps her hands and starts a takedown chant. Now our whole side of the bleachers is chanting at Doug. "Take-down!" Clap, clap, clap. "Take-down!" Clap, clap, clap. "Take-down!" Clap, clap, clap.

Both Doug and the L.C. guy shoot for the takedown at the same time. They bump heads and go to the mat. Doug gets the worst of it and L.C. slips behind for the points. Smith and I look at each other.

"Come on, you Dougie!" Randy yells. "Put it on 'im! Gobble, gobble, gobble one time!"

Doug looks sheepishly to the bench where Coach

Ratta and the assistant coach, Tom Morgan, sit with the JVs. Morgan laughs and speaks into the tape recorder.

L.C. has visions of a quick pin. He begins to ride Doug high, looking to sneak a half-nelson on him and drive him to his back. Doug feels the guy's weight shifting and lets him have the half-nelson. Almost. The light of five pinning points shines in his eyes as L.C. starts to drive Doug over. Doug clamps down hard on the guy's feeble half-nelson, rolls to his back, then right over again. Our bleachers erupt in a chant of "Pin, pin, pin!" and the light in L.C.'s eyes turn to panic. He flops and strains and tries to bridge, but Doug has his shoulders controlled now with a half-nelson of his own. Slap! The ref slaps the mat, and it's all over. Our side cheers, the L.C. side sighs, and Doug bounces up and waits for the ref to raise his hand.

There it is: balance again. The most important quality a wrestler has. More important than strength, speed, smarts—even more important than endurance. You *feel* the guy's weight. You *feel* where he's going, what his body's going to do. Then you take advantage. You use his strength, his speed, his smarts, even his endurance, against him.

I'm not terribly excited about the other JV matches, so I go sit with Kuch and Sausage. Kuch is trying to bolster Sausage's confidence. Mash did a little psych job on him at the weigh-in. Mash knew he couldn't make weight with his warm-up suit on, but he tried anyway. The ref read off 104 1/2. You could just see Sausage thinking, "He's not gonna make weight! I won't be killed!" Mash took off his warm-ups. In his tights and top he weighed 103 1/4. Sausage closed his eyes, undoubtedly calculating the weight of an L.C. wrestling uniform. Mash stripped to his jock. Sausage peeked around the ref and read the results for himself. 102 3/4. He turned a whiter shade of pale.

Mash stood off by himself and put his stuff back on. With no larger person next to him to put his small stature in perspective, Mash looks like he could go about nine feet three and 690 pounds. Sausage shouldn't have looked, but he did.

"You gotta go after him, Sausage," Kuch says. "You've got nothing to lose. Go out there fierce and proud and there's no way you'll come back ashamed. No matter how bad ya get beat."

Sausage is hunched up in a corner. He hangs his head between his legs and breathes heavily through his mouth.

Balldozer comes over, pats him on the knee, and says, "Shit to the thirteenth power, Sausage," which is a French way of saying good luck.

Coach comes through the door smiling. The JVs pulled it out, 22–19. He tells us, like he always does, that we'll have a minute of silence before we head out.

Schmoozler turns off his James Taylor tape. Jerry and Mike Konigi, who are Buddhists, pray. So do Seeley and Williamson and Smith and Raska, who are what they call "born-again" Christians.

I really like it that none of the religious guys on the team evangelizes any more. Coach, who is a Christian, gives a talk at the start of the season about peoples' rights to their views of life. He had to start doing it in my sophomore year because there got to be so much conflict among born-agains and heads and guys who just wanted to be left alone to wrestle that it wasn't hardly any fun to come to practice.

Once I asked Coach what he prayed about in our minute of silence and he said he thanked God for the gift of life and prayed that nobody got hurt too bad.

Sausage, I'm sure, usually spends his silent minute dreaming of at least a hand job after the match. I doubt his thoughts are on his cock this evening, though. He and Kuch are huddled in the corner and Kuch is whispering softly. I know exactly what he's saying:

"Even if my people must eventually pass from the face of the earth, they will live on in whatever men are fierce and strong, so that when women see a man who is proud and brave and vengeful, even if he has a white face, they will cry: 'That is a Human Being!' "

I never know what Balldozer is thinking. I really like him, but with his French and Brazilian backgrounds, we have some kind of cultural gap.

Schmooz is pillowed up on his warm-up jacket, singing softly, "In my mind I'm gone to Carolina. . . ." I can see his lips move.

Otto's got his feet up on the wall and behind his closed eyes he's watching films on the ceiling. He's only thinking of the way to win. Before a wrestling match or a football game Otto becomes cybernetic. Name a move and he tells you the counter. Name a play and he tells you his assignment. "Guy goes for a single leg, I go for a whizzer. Thirty-four-trap: I pull and rip their tackle at the line, then look for the linebacker."

I'm not thinking much of anything.

Lewis and Clark is about finished with their exercises. They're the only team that doesn't run out on the mat. They walk out real slow, swaying druidically in their black hooded warm-up suits. Their hoods come down so far you can't see their faces. Mash leads the way. They look like mean lumps of coal, except for Romaine Lewis. He's tall and slim and his hood won't fit over his hair. He wears it in dread knots and looks like a mean black male Medusa. And L.C. doesn't shout out their exercises. They just grunt and moan a little at each other. Opposing schools' fans get very offended. There's something of the air of professional wrestling in their histrionics. They do it to psych out their opponents and it works about half the time. It sure works on me. I love it so much I just want to applaud. It takes me until my second round before I even feel like serious wrestling. Roman Polanski would love the L.C. warm-ups.

We're all bunched up behind the locker-room door. Coach has left us and gone out to the bench to chuckle at L.C. Sausage is on tiptoes, peering through the little window in the door to see when they finish. He's all set to lead us out on the mat and take us through our exercises.

"Okay," Sausage says. He turns back to face us. He takes a big breath. The captain is always supposed to give a big battle cry as we charge out.

"Dog style!" yells Sausage as we burst through the door to heavy cheers and thread our way between the bleachers to the mat. We're all sprinting, legs high, and whooping hard and laughing a little, too, at Sausage's chilling call to arms. I'd say he's in the right frame of mind.

We're fairly loose and sweating just a bead or two by the end of the exercises. Sausage leads us a couple times around the big gold circle as we whoop and holler, then to the bench.

In a minute we're out on the mat again for the introductions. The two teams line up, facing each other. The announcer gives the weight class, then introduces the wrestlers. Sausage has only a black apparition with which to shake hands. But we know Mash is in there. He moves like a small but mighty thunderhead back to the L.C. bench to take off his warm-up suit and do a few more twists and bends. Coach takes Konigi and Sausage back behind our bench and kneads their shoulders in turn and

135

talks steadily to them. Romaine gives me a couple fists to bang. I do it twice.

"Brother man," he says and bangs back once.

"Good luck, Romaine," I reply. I sure like him. As long as we've been acquainted I've always wanted to get to know him better. Go camping or to some shows or something. Otto knows him pretty well. Romaine is a wide receiver and defensive halfback.

Little Konigi decisions his man in a crummy match characterized by mutual stalling. He got two takedown points and then wrestled defensively the rest of the match. His older brother yells at him by the drinking fountain. They're a funny pair. Little Konig is a hellraiser everywhere but on the mat, where he's technically good enough but wrestles like he's signed a nonaggression pact. Big Konig is shy everywhere but on the mat, where he goes for broke every second. His matches never go beyond two rounds. It's pin or get pinned for the Big Konig at 123.

The ref signals for Mash and Sausage. Sausage trots out like a little pony. Mash takes his time. They meet in the inner gold circle, shake hands, and turn to face each other. The ref blows his whistle.

Down goes Sausage after a single leg. Mash counters with a cross-face that bends Sausage's nose about 180 degrees, then shoves him away. Sausage's headgear is pushed over his eyes, so the ref calls time.

Down goes Sausage to sweep a leg. Mash is too fast and Sausage sweeps air.

Sausage locks up like the pro wrestlers on TV. He stands forehead to forehead with Mash and tries to muscle. Each has a hand behind the other's neck and a hand on the other's elbow. Our bench goes wild. "You can't muscle him, Turd Head!" Schmoozler yells. Coach Morgan talks into the tape recorder.

Sausage is pushing Mash around the mat. Mash, of course, is letting him, inviting Sausage to precipitate his own demise. Balance again. Our crowd loves Sausage's aggressiveness and cheers like crazy.

Kuch taps my knee. "Look," he says. I was watching Mr. and Mrs. Mashamura. They sit as calm as can be. Smiling intently is the furthest they seem to go emotionally. Mash has hooked both of Sausage's arms. Sausage is hopelessly off balance but pumps his legs hard and drives his head into Mash's navel just the same. Mash suddenly kicks out both legs. Sausage is smashed flat. His nose is taking quite a beating.

Sausage barks and wheezes a little and tries to get up, but Mash has spun behind him for two points. Sausage is right to his knees like a shot, crawling around the mat in a burst of energy. Mash can't find anything to grab. The buzzer sounds and the Sausage Man has survived round one.

Sausage gets his choice of positions and chooses top. The ref is down on one knee looking Mash in the eye. Sausage sights along Mash's spine and stares into the barrel of the ref's whistle. It blows.

Mash kicks into a beautiful long sit-out. Sausage grabs for him, but he's long gone with his escape point.

Mash is more aggressive on his feet this round. He acts like he wants to lock up, but when Sausage reaches for him, Mash drops to one knee and takes Sausage to his back with a fireman's carry. Immediately he gets the half-nelson, then the crotch. Sausage has had it. Mash lifts a little on the crotch and the leverage pushes both Sausage's shoulders deep into the mat. He's pinned. We don't even have time to yell for him to bridge before the ref slaps the mat. The L.C. fans jump up cheering.

All of a sudden Sausage's dad is out of the bleachers and onto the mat, yelling at the ref. Coach is off the bench and between them fast. Mr. Thuringer is pointing at the ref and trying to get at him, yelling that the whistle was too fast. Sausage is up and between Coach and his dad, trying to shove his dad off the mat. Both benches are paralyzed, but the L.C. fans hoot and jeer. This kind of stuff doesn't happen very often.

Mr. Thuringer realizes right away what an ass he is—you can see it come over his face. He says something to Sausage and Sausage pats him on the back. Instead of just going back and sitting down, he apologizes to Coach and the ref and then to Mash right there on the mat. I can't hear what he's saying because the L.C. fans are yelling so loud. But it's obvious he's apologizing.

The ref raises Mash's hand and then Mash goes over and puts his arm around Sausage and talks to him and his dad for a few seconds. Then he sprints back to his bench and they mob him joyfully.

We all get up and meet Sausage, who is crying and smiling both. Coach Morgan puts his arm around him and takes him behind the bench to fix his nose.

Raska and Mike Konigi win, Seeley gets beat by a point in a great match, Schmoozler tears his guy a couple new assholes but can't pin him, Williamson loses bad, and Kuch is up 5–0 in the first round when I get up and walk behind the bench to loosen up for my match.

Carla got here in time to see Schmooz dig a few furrows across the mat with Steve Munkers's head. Schmooz would drive him to his back and almost have him pinned; then Munkers would bridge way up on the back of his head and scoot off the mat. They'd go back to the referee's position and the same thing would happen. Schmooz would drive hard at the whistle and Munkers would go to his back. Then he'd bridge and Schmooz would drive and off the mat they'd go. It was like a ritual. The crowd loved it. I'd hate to have to trade scalps with

Munkers. The back of his head will be all scabs tomorrow.

Carla trots over, pats my arm, smiles big, and tells me good luck. Then she goes back to her seat beside Belle. Belle saves her a seat when Carla comes late from work. A couple maladjusted creeps in the L.C. section yell out how cute it is that I have a girl friend. They really love it when I begin my rope-skipping. A few of the older men hoot and yell out, "Hey, Sugar Ray!" I hear it all.

Kuch is about to pin Rance Prokoff, so I whip the rope faster. I reverse the rope a few times and start to blow the air out hard. If they were not so concerned about their guy being smothered by Kuch's braid, the L.C. crowd would be on my ass for sure. They're screaming at the ref, whose only concern is Rance's shoulders. Kuch is coiled around Rance like a vine, stretching him out with a hold called a "guillotine." It's hard to tell who's the one in trouble unless you know the hold. They're both on their backs, wrapped head to toe, but Kuch's arm is woven under Rance's neck, around his shoulder, and under his back, where Kuch's hands are locked. The higher Rance bridges, the more Kuch stretches him and the closer Rance's free shoulder is drawn to the mat. Rance is straining hard to pull away and wagging his head back and forth, trying to shake off Kuch's thick braid, which is probably annoying but definitely not overwhelming. Coach Morgan runs out and flips it off. Our fans boo and their fans yell at our fans.

Romaine is behind their bench, stretching his groin and looking over at me. I dance a little and reverse the rope some more. I turn a little circle while I skip. The rope whacks the warm-up mat steadily.

Kuch almost has him, but the whistle blows, ending the round. That gives me more time.

139

I'm bridging on my neck, working it around and around, when the pinning chant begins. I can't make it to my feet before I hear the ref slap the mat. Kuch has Rance stacked up in a beautiful chicken wing just like Coach demonstrated on Balldozer in practice. It takes them a few seconds to get untangled. I put my jump rope under my chair and walk with the guys to the edge of the mat to congratulate Kuch. He's smiling and not even breathing hard.

"Way t' go," I say.

"See ya soon," he replies.

You can barely hear the announcer through all the noise. Cheers and boos and stomping feet. I'm the least popular wrestler in Spokane. Also, along with Shute, I'm the most popular. It depends on who you talk to. Some people don't like it that I dance and skip rope.

Romaine and I cross, shake hands, and turn to face each other. Romaine glares. He's into being tough on the mat. Only a real cretin is psyched-out by that kind of shit. The ref's whistle chirps. I hear Kuch yip and howl like a coyote.

I stand straight and bounce a little on my toes. Romaine is crouched and moving slowly forward. I seem heavier, but he outweighs me by seven pounds. His arms are so long he's hard to lock up with. And he's so tall it's hard to take him down with leg dives.

He taps my forehead and I bounce away. He's after me, trying to lock up or maybe work an arm drag—catch one of my arms and pull me forward off balance so he can slip inside and get a leg. His hand whips out and slaps the side of my head. Part of the tough-guy routine. Our fans boo and theirs cheer. I bounce away and dance a little and stand straight.

His hand whips out again, but I duck, drop to one

knee, and sweep his leg, hoisting it high as I move behind him. I trip the other leg and he goes down. I get the two points and our crowd cheers.

Because he's tall, I work on controlling his crotch. Most of his strength is in his legs, so I ride him low, my arm locked back around his hips and through his crotch rather than around his waist, my leg hooked through his at the knee. Romaine is really a tough guy. I never liked playing against him in football and I'd run away from him in a street fight. But for a wrestler he has poor balance. You ride his hips tight and you know right where he's going. He doesn't try much except to get back to his feet. I ride him out to the whistle.

Romaine chooses top. I get down on my hands and knees in the referee's position and Romaine gets down beside me and grabs hold. The ref checks our position and my nose begins to bleed. Just a couple drops at first. But it's a steady stream by the time he moves back and sticks his whistle in his mouth. He calls time and motions to our bench. Tommy Reilly, our manager, runs out with the wet towel to wipe the blood off the mat. I pass him on my way to the bench to meet Coach.

"I didn't even get hit," I say apologetically.

Coach wipes my nose and mouth. "Better go all out this round, Louden," he says as he stuffs the little gauze stoppers in.

I nod. I can taste the blood. I breathe through my mouth and the blood bubbles. I swallow it.

"Come on, you Swain, take him now!" yells Otto.

I sit out at the whistle. Romaine can't stay with me and I escape for a point. I go right after him. He reaches to lock up and I drag his arm. I take him to his knees and get control for two points. The ref calls time. Romaine's back is covered with my blood.

I pass Tommy again walking to the bench. I get one more time-out before I'm disqualified.

"Have to do it pretty soon, son," Coach says. He lays me down on my back and presses both thumbs along the bridge of my nose between my eyes. Things go a little black. He stuffs my nose full of stoppers and pats me on the back.

I drive hard at the whistle, but Romaine stays steady on his hands and knees. I go for the half-nelson and he counters by going to his feet. I lift him up with an arm through the crotch and bring him back to the mat hard. Too hard. The ref blows his whistle and gives Romaine a penalty point. The L.C. fans cheer and jeer at me. Some people also think I'm mean. But I'm not. Our fans boo. I apologize and Romaine taps my fists with his.

We're both on our feet now. My nose is dripping when the whistle blows. I fake a lock-up and dive for a leg. Romaine is ready. I don't get much of a hold and he comes with a cross-face that bends my head back and makes me release the leg and go back to my feet. Blood's all down my top and onto my tights. Romaine hesitates and looks at the ref. He blows his whistle and motions to our bench.

The L.C. crowd has flipped out. They're jumping up and down and pounding each other on the back. Our crowd is pretty quiet. I could lose my first match in two and a half years if my platelets don't start promoting some coagulation. I'm aware of it, but I'm not self-conscious or scared. I'm wrestling the best I can.

Coach puts the pressure on my nose again. "Get him to lock up, then take your fireman's carry," he says.

"Okay," I nod. The pressure on my nose feels good. I breathe deep and slow through my mouth.

Our bench and crowd yell me a lot of support when I walk back to the circle. L.C. is screaming for Romaine.

I get a little look at Carla, calm and smiling.

I don't really hear the whistle. Romaine starts for me slowly and I just wait. He reaches for an arm, but I pull away. I look up at the clock. There's a minute left in the round and I think about stalling it out. I move forward and Romaine moves to meet me. We lock up loosely. I back away a bit, then blast forward, hooking his arm and dropping for the leg. I pull him over my shoulders and slam him down, maybe too hard. But there's no whistle. I go for the half-nelson and crotch as Romaine tries to roll on his side. I cinch up good on the half-nelson and keep him on his back. I kick my legs out wide and get up on my toes to be just as heavy on his chest as I can. I lift on his head and crotch and press down with my chest. His jersey is covered with blood. I can't hear a thing the crowd is so loud. I close my eyes and sink the half-nelson deeper and cinch up with all I've got. A tremendous cheer bursts from somewhere. A hand taps my back and I let loose and roll off Romaine and onto my back, swallowing blood.

The ref motions for me to get up. Romaine and I shake hands and then the ref raises my arm. I turn toward the bench and see the clock with just six seconds left. Everybody's waiting for me at the edge of the mat.

XIX

I'm so goddamn tired of spinach. I called Dr. Livengood after the match and told him about my nose. He said I wasn't getting enough iron and that I should eat spinach and cream of wheat. I can't eat cream of wheat because it's too much bulk, so I'm eating spinach. God, I hate it. I've got spinach breath, my teeth are turning green, and I've become estranged from my own stools they're so ugly and malodorous. And it's only been two days.

One good thing, though: I've only had one bloody nose. Dad accidentally whacked me with a cold turkey leg as he was getting it out of the frig. I was standing behind him, reminiscing about what an eating orgy Christmas vacation used to be for me, when WHAM—I get this big, brown, greasy turkey leg right square on my beleaguered schnozzola. It only bled a little.

Dad was really sorry. I pretended to attack him to get at the turkey leg and he pretended to beat me with it. Carla laughed and Katzen ran downstairs to her bear. I was about semigory with blood and turkey grease when Kuch and Otto came to pick me up to run. We ran early tonight so we could get plenty of sleep. The turkey smell was so luscious I hated to wash my face. The bus leaves for Missoula at five tomorrow evening.

When I got back I banged the door open with a shoulder block and stood in the doorway kicking snow off my boots. We put new weather stripping on the doors this winter. You have to be Larry Csonka to open the things.

"How ya doin'?" Dad asked. He sat by the fire reading *Time* in poor light.

"Fine, Dad," I replied, shaking the ice out of my hair. Instead of running I walked home from the park, so the melted snow froze on me. I grabbed the towel that I tuck around the neck of my rubber sweat suit and wiped my head and face.

Carla came upstairs. She walked very slowly because Katzen was perched on her shoulder, peeking precariously through the swirls of her hair.

"How about some spinach?" Carla asked.

"No, thanks," I replied. "I don't need that much iron. I wouldn't want to rust before I wrestle Shute."

I whipped downstairs and took a quick shower and returned in a clean pair of old sweat pants. Carla sat on the floor in front of the fire and Katzen slept curled on Dad's *Time* in his lap. Between the fragrance of the Christmas tree and the pine-scented candle I gave Carla, the living room smelled like the woods.

Dad was trying to push some Christmas candy on Carla. He's a great one for lots of goodies at Christmastime. It's like the old thing about the poor kid who makes good and wants his family to have the stuff he didn't. In Dad's case the cliché is real. I've seen the cabin he lived in—the foundation of it, anyway. And I've walked most of the two miles he walked to the highway to catch the school bus. Part of that walk is under water now. I've seen pictures of him in his Sunday best—his sweat shirt, his black jeans, and his weird high shoes with the huge round toes. Dad's hair was jet black and straight then. His complexion is darker than mine and his cheekbones are high. In one of his old basketball pictures he looks like an Indian. His hair is wavy now and gray around the ears. He said he pressed the wave into it when he was fishing in Alaska before he went into the service. In his Alaska pictures he's got one of those little thin mustaches and looks exactly like the old movie star Clark Gable. I try to get him to grow it again, but he won't.

Every Christmas Dad always got Mom and me about a dozen presents each. Perfume and scented soap and slippers and robes and tapes for her, always socks and gloves and a flannel shirt and whatever I needed for school or sports. I don't think he got Mom anything this year, though. But he got Carla and me all kinds of stuff.

I think it really hurts him that I'm not able to eat my way through the holidays this year. Otto takes up the slack. This evening he was good for a few chocolate peanuts for his pockets, a couple pieces of fudge, a slice of cold turkey, and a big mouthful of hard candy to keep his energy level high through our three miles. Kuch went for a glass of cider.

Dad likes Otto. Otto reminds Dad of himself as a kid. I can see it in his face. Otto doesn't have much money and neither did Dad. Otto's parents broke up when he was pretty young and so did Dad's. Otto's got it a little tougher than Dad had it, though. At least as far as I know. Otto's been living with his father in an apartment downtown since his mother was committed to the state hospital for her alcoholism. I used to stop by his place on my way home from work, until one night when just before I knocked on the window of their apartment, I heard Mr.

Lafte yelling at Otto that he was just a big fat baby and not as tough as he thought. He was drunk and I could hear him push Otto after each sentence. "Oh, come on, Dad. Jesus Christ, lay off!" was about all Otto said back. I wanted to leave, out of respect for Otto, but my curiosity got the best of me, and I walked quietly up to their half-open door. Mr. Lafte, who is nearly as big as Otto but about half dead from straight whiskey and three packs of Camels a day, kept pushing and pushing. He's already had some of his throat removed because of cancer and his voice bubbles with phlegm. He began slap-fighting with Otto, boxing him around the room. Finally, Otto yelled, "Goddamnit, Dad!" and shoved him across the room, past the door, and into a wooden table, which shattered with a crash. Mr. Lafte got up swearing and swinging. Through the open door I saw him rush across the room. Then I ran away. Otto is as gentle a guy as could be to his friends and to everybody who doesn't give him shit. But he's vicious with people he thinks do him or his friends wrong. Then he fights crazy, like a dog. Dad sold Otto his '58 Chevy at cost. That and his letter sweater are the only nice things Otto has. If Otto didn't have sports to make a career and maybe to channel his meanness, I'd be worried about his future.

I'd love to munch some candy with Dad. I could probably handle a piece or two. I'm holding 147 pretty well now. It's just that eating trash food after all this time would spoil the pattern. It would upset the rhythm I've got going with my body and break the deal I made with my spirit. I mean, I'm so close now I can see the end.

I really feel like I understand that Franz Kafka story "A Hunger Artist" now. It's about this guy who's into fasting as a profession. He's making a good living at it until somebody invents the radio or something and everybody turns elsewhere for entertainment. He should hang it up and move into some other line, but he doesn't. He's become an artist of hunger. What was once a painful discipline has become fulfilling and beautiful just for its own sake. His manager tries to get him to quit, but it's too late. The Hunger Artist just fasts himself into a pile of dusty satisfaction at the bottom of his cage. I can't say there's a real strict correlation between the two of us. I mean, I'm not quite ready for cosmic union. But I think I finally do understand what Kafka was getting at.

Dad popped a couple gumdrop orange slices into his mouth and Carla grabbed a miniature candy cane to suck. "Good candy," Dad said. He put a little bit of gumdrop on Katzen's nose. She slept away, not even flinching. "See," Dad said smiling, "even my cat likes it."

Carla's asleep after a load of love that should hold us over the two days I'll be in Montana. I should be asleep, too, but I'm just too excited, so I'm sitting here in the basement living room in front of a little fire I just made in the fireplace. In five days I'll wrestle Shute and end four months of working toward it. Then we've got test week at school, I turn in my senior thesis, and it's all over. It feels funny to know it's ending. The whole semester has been a little strange because of that. Spring semester will probably be that way for kids graduating at the end of the year. You see things in a special way when you realize your days among them are numbered. You try to treat people a little different so you can leave them with the truest impression of what they've meant to you. I could always go back and hang around school like some guys do after they graduate, but I don't want to do that. I'll visit Gene and Leeland and Coach, but I want to make this break a clean one. I want to put the high school part of my life behind me.

Carla and I and Dad and Cindy and Willa watched the

old version of *A Christmas Carol* on TV a few nights ago, and although I didn't bring it up, I was really impressed by this idea of seeing the end of things in that story. I mean it's Scrooge's knowledge of the end of things that changes his life. Those ghosts show him a glimpse of the future and it gives him a new perspective. Then he takes charge of himself and changes. It takes supernatural power to make old Scrooge realize something everybody should know just from looking around: that he's going to die. This idea of realizing your death and accepting it and keeping its realization with you always is the major thing I got out of Carlos Castaneda's books about his days with Don Juan. This awareness and acceptance of death sets up an almost contradictory way of looking at life. On the one hand, you know your time is short, so you use it preciously. Then on the other hand, you know it all comes to dust anyway, so you don't value anything too highly. You have things in a perspective that allows you to live in equilibrium with the universe. I've tried and tried to find a way to work *A Christmas Carol* into my senior thesis, but it's almost done now and I'd wreck it if I tried to stick something new in. I've got the Castaneda stuff all through it.

You can't graduate with honors from David Thompson unless you write a senior thesis. At the end of the school year the Honor Society has a meeting in which they tell the juniors about the thesis and hand out a little booklet of instructions. That gives you the summer and most of your senior year to get it done. The thesis is supposed to be long and serious and it has to pass a panel of teachers, so you really do need some time. Washington state colleges are supposed to dig David Thompson graduates because of our theses. Tanneran, who is my thesis advisor, says colleges are hurting so bad for students now he doubts if they give a fuck if the kids they admit are even literate. I decided to write the thing not so much to make my record look good as just to wind up my high school time having done everything there was to do. From the time I was in grade school Dad would take me to all the David Thompson games in all the sports. I'd hang around the football field and the gym watching all the practices, wanting so bad to be big and go to David Thompson. It became what they call a ruling passion.

I should be typing, but it's fun just to sit here and look into the fire. Besides, I'd wake up Carla. The thesis has to have footnotes and a bibliography and it's got to have a conclusion all my own. The conclusion is all I've got left to do, and then I've got to type the whole mess. I'm just lucky I happened on my topic real early, or else with work and working-out extra hard, I'd never have gotten it done. It's called "The Mean Goodness" and it's about the meaning of life. I figured since it was such an important assignment I wouldn't mess around with trivialities. The title comes from the first piece we read in senior English.

The first day of class Tanneran came in wearing jeans, a white tennis shirt, and a gray tweed sport coat, sat on the desk, and said slow and cretinistically, "Ahm gonner teach yawl ta read." Then he smiled and we saw he'd blacked out about half his teeth so they looked like they were missing. People laughed a little. Then Thurston Reilly, editor of the school paper, said, "But we knows how ta read!"

"I don't think you do! I do not think you do!" Gene said in his normal voice. He passed out copies of James Agee's "Knoxville: Summer 1915" and told us to read it and be ready to talk about it the next day. Then he left and didn't come back.

We were all seniors and figured we damn sure knew

how to read. A couple kids were offended, but most of us were just dumbfounded. Some people left and some stayed and read it. After about thirty-five minutes Reilly turned to me and said, "This is grounds for an editorial." And he walked out with a gleam in his eye.

The next morning before school started Reilly found me in the gym and showed me his editorial. He is by far the best editor *The David Thompson Explorer* has had since I've been here and it looked like he'd scored again. The title was "Senior English—the Same Old Hype." It described young, hairy teachers with old, crew-cut ideas. He worked some cute stuff with "hype" and "hip" and "hypocritical." I didn't get to read it all because I was dripping sweat on it and he grabbed it away.

Tanneran was a few minutes late to class. Everybody asked everybody else what they thought the Agee piece was about. I thought I knew maybe a little of what it was about, because it seemed to fit so well into my thesis, which I'd been working at since June. But in typical wise-ass fashion I said, "Well, I think it's a surrealist, paranoid vision of how the Army deals with indecent exposure," and I quoted the line ". . . the urination of huge children stood loosely military against an invisible wall. . . ." I got no reaction, except from Molly Philabaum, who gave me the finger. Molly never could take a joke. Last year when Kuch was into his Indian phase and I was in my doctor phase, I hung out my shingle on my locker:

THE DOCTOR IS IN
HYMENECTOMIES WHILE YOU WAIT!

Molly tore it down and reported me to the vice-principal. He at least understood the humor. Everybody knows the only market for hymenectomies is junior high.

Gene came in and asked the class what the piece was about. Nobody said anything. Gene walked back to his chair, sat down, spread his arms and legs wide, flopped his head over, and pretended to snooze. In about ten minutes he opened an eye and scanned the room. Molly was the first to light into him about the stupid assignment and how it didn't relate at all to our lives.

"Molly . . . ?" Gene asked as he got up and stood in front of us. He was sharp in his heavy suede pants, thick old suspenders, and red and black plaid shirt. "Molly, you're never going to die?"

Nobody said anything. I suppressed an urge to say Molly smelled like she was already dead. Molly should be introduced to feminine hygiene. That's what happens when they make P.E. optional.

Then Gene quoted these lines. People always have at least a measure of confidence in a good quoter:

"By some chance here we are, all on this earth; and who shall ever tell the sorrow of being on this earth, lying, on quilts, on the grass, in a summer evening, among the sounds of night. May God bless my people, my uncle, my aunt, my mother, my good father, oh remember them kindly in their time of trouble; and in the hour of their taking away."

"Okay," he said. "Who knows what Agee's talking about in this piece?"

" 'The sorrow of being on this earth,' " answered Patty Ryder in a flash.

"And what is sorrowful about being on this earth?" Gene asked.

" 'The hour of their taking away,' " shot back Larry Brooks. Our class ain't dumb.

I was thinking of old David Thompson back when he was the first white man to set eyes on the Columbia River. And I wondered to myself how, how could he ever have imagined when he named that river that there

152

would ever be enough power on earth to turn it into a fucking lake.

"*Our* taking away," added Reilly.

"I don't think quite that," Gene replied. "Not just that. Let's look at everything Agee says. Everything." Then he went up to the board and wrote "Every Single Word."

"Knoxville: Summer 1915" is only four pages long, but we read it for the next three days. Each of us read a few lines over and over aloud until we could say what they meant literally and how they fit in with the whole thing. We agreed it was a piece worth reading and that we couldn't make a fair judgment on it at first because we couldn't understand it.

Reading it over so much is how I came up with the title of my thesis. It comes from this line:

> These sweet pale streamings in the light lift out their pallors and their voices all together, mothers hushing their children, the hushing unnaturally prolonged, the men gentle and silent and each snail-like withdrawn into the quietude of what he singly is doing, the urination of huge children stood loosely military against an invisible wall, and gentle happy and peaceful, tasting the mean goodness of their living like the last of their suppers in their mouths.

Dinner is over and all the families in the neighborhood are out on their lawns. The fathers are watering the grass with hoses, the kids are playing, and the mothers are feeling the men's tranquillity at being home from work, I guess, because Agee says the way they hush the children is "unnaturally prolonged." Just a bunch of middle- or lower-middle-class people enjoying their tiny pieces of the universe. The lots these guys live on might only be fifty feet wide, but they water the lawn with as much pride as they'd take in watering the lawn of a mansion.

153

More, probably, because if they owned mansions they'd have gardeners or sprinkling systems.

Agee describes the men as huge children peeing because that's probably how he remembers thinking of men with hoses. That's how I still think of a guy with a hose. He describes them as "loosely military against an invisible wall" maybe because he thinks living is like being sentenced to a firing squad without knowing where or when you're going to be lined up against the wall. This makes sense to me. I mean, we're born and the guns cock. Once the guns are cocked they can go off any time.

I'm not sure why the men are "gentle happy and peaceful." Maybe they feel the beauty of being with their families, watering a patch of grass on a beautiful evening, is as much beauty as life offers condemned men. If this is what Agee's getting at, then "tasting the mean goodness of their living" means that the men understand or at least feel the meaning of life. "Good" because it feels good. "Mean" because it feels so good you want it to last forever.

In the back of the bus the younger guys giggle and light farts and pretend to beat off. It's going to be a long two days, so I'm here in front, taking a seminap. The older you get, the more toward the front of the bus you seem to go, until you're right up here in front with Coach. I also like the fresh air coming under the door. My nose gets dry if I can't get a little fresh air blowing in my face.

It's not quite daylight yet, but most everybody seems awake. Kuch is reading *Motocross* magazine, Schmooz has the New Riders' "Dirty Business" going softly on his tape player, and Otto is looking out over the Spokane River. The closer it gets to daylight, the more the river reflects the mountains. They seem to be growing right out of the snow banks into the gray water. Coach snores lightly under his old hunting hat. He's got the ear flaps down and reminds me of pictures I've seen of Chinese farmers in the wintertime. Except he's Japanese.

The Missoula trip is the big road trip of the season because everybody gets to go. The varsity has two matches, the JV has two, and everybody else gets lined up against somebody close to his weight. Our JVs wrestle Custer at two this afternoon. That's why we had to leave so early. We wrestle until it's time for the Lewis and Clark–Battleground matches in the evening. Then tomorrow the losing teams wrestle each other in the afternoon and the winners go in the evening. It's really fun.

"Hey, Louden." From behind I hear a muffled summons. It's Norty Wheeler, crawling up the aisle on all fours. He looks spaced. His eyes bristle. He's just dropped from heavyweight to 185 so he can go first-man JV against Custer. Otto and Howard Fontaine have beaten Norty consistently for the number-one and number-two heavyweight spots, but he dropped to 185 and whipped up on Craig Martin for number two there. Then Balldozer thrashed Norty so bad in their wrestle-off for number one that Norty may be disoriented still.

"Hi, Norty," I say.

Otto turns from the window. "Mornin', Dog Breath" is his greeting for Nort.

"Wuff, wuff " is Nort's reply.

"What's wrong, Nort?" I ask. "Ya look bad." He's wearing a red double-knit tie. The part that should be short is longer than the long part and it flops out of his letter sweater like a thin tongue. He lettered in football, which is not bad for a sophomore at David Thompson.

"I got no norms," Norty whines. "And also I'm hungry."

"What don't you have, Nort?" asks Otto.

"Norms. I got no norms. None of us do. Mr. Borison says we live in a time of anomie." Borison teaches sociology.

"Swain's got some norms," replies Otto. "I saw 'em yesterday in the shower."

"Think of it this way, Nort," I console. "You've got a lot of abnorms."

"You guys are a comfort," he replies. "Got anything to eat?" He droops in Saint Bernard style.

"You didn't bring anything?" I'm astounded.

"Cake and turkey sandwiches," Nort replies. "But nothin' I can eat before the match. I'd never make weight. I think I'm on some kind of Nutrament high. I drank a can on the way to school and I feel a little spacy."

"You look like shit," interjects Otto.

Norty's blood sugar is probably low. I reach for my honey bottle. "Open up," I say. I squeeze a thick golden line of honey onto his tongue.

"Ummmmm, good." Nort smiles. He turns around and crawls back toward the rear.

Otto and I look at each other. "Hypoglycemic," I say.

"Poor fucker's got no norms," Otto replies.

The bus driver pumps the brakes. We slide just a little at first, then straighten out and slow down. Out the window on our side red and blue lights flash and twirl. A pickup with a big camper is stuck up to the hubs in the entrance to a little roadside park. A state trooper and a couple wrecker guys stand around. Nobody seems to be hurt or anything. An old couple sit in the cab of the pickup. The bus driver pours it on again.

"Guy must have tried to pull in there for a snooze," I observe. "Must have thought he was driving a snow vehicle."

"Fuck," says Otto. He shivers. "Every time we take a road trip we see an accident or something."

I know what Otto's thinking about, but I don't respond. He turns and watches Idaho go by outside the window and I close my eyes.

We were really into violence and meanness our sophomore year. Me and Otto and Kuch. We had to be to make varsity on a state championship team. Few of the older guys liked us because we were so insane. Running guys into the walls in wrestle-offs if we couldn't do anything else to shake them loose. Screaming and dancing and never stopping brutalizing ourselves and anybody else we got our hands on. We each won our first match, against Marcus Whitman, and we were about psyched to our crania for the next ones, which were against Grand Coulee and Chief Joseph in a triangular meet at Chief Joseph in Wenatchee. We were doubly psyched because it was our first road trip.

We had to leave real early to make Wenatchee by noon. Everybody was asleep by the time we turned up the ramp for 90 West. Everybody except Otto and Kuch and me. Spokane looked really neat from Sunset Hill. Downtown had just been decorated for Christmas and we could see the Christmas lights there and a few others that had been left on all night in the residential neighborhoods. We scanned the Northside of town and spotted the water tower. You can see the tower easily from Sunset Hill at night and you can just make out the high school. It felt good to be part of all the David Thompson green and gold.

Just outside of Cheney a couple state troopers screamed by us, fishtailing like crazy on the black ice. The sirens woke everybody and from the front of the bus guys were yelling about a fire up the road. By the time we crossed the railroad tracks the road in front of us was all lit up in firelight. The three of us looked out the side windows but couldn't see anything except patrol cars and a couple Cheney fire trucks until a trooper waved us to the shoulder and around the fire trucks. The bus driver swung out and around and got stuck. Then we could see what was going on, because the back windows looked right between the two fire trucks and square at the wreck. A gas truck was jackknifed across the highway, and a VW sedan had rammed into the side of it right where the gas valves were. The fire trucks were spraying foam all over, but still rivers of fire a yard wide ran across the road. A body hung out the driver's window. It was part black and part covered with foam. The hair burst into flames right before our eyes. Another body twitched and danced in the flames on the passenger side. The head was nearly severed and lolled out the window. I guess it was the trachea that waved in the boiling flames.

The bus driver spun the wheels and rocked the bus back and forth. Everybody rushed mad-assed to the back of the bus to see. Guys were smashing me against the window. The head that was almost cut off seemed to be screaming, but of course it wasn't. The window started to get awful hot against my cheek, but then one of the fire trucks turned the foam on us and it covered the window. Everybody got off me since there wasn't anything to see any more. The bus started getting hot, so Coach had some guys open all the windows on the side away from the fire. We could hear the flames bellowing like the wind. When a couple of the truck tires exploded, somebody yelled that the truck was about to explode, too. Oh, fuck, I thought. I stood up in panic and got ready to dive out a window. But the snow was melting all around and the bus tires had dug down to bare ground and spun us back onto the highway.

I don't think anybody but Kuch and Otto and me got a very good look, with the bus rocking and everybody pushing and all. It didn't seem like anybody else did, because we were the only ones not talking about how neat it was. It turned Otto straight to stone and Kuch and I just looked back and forth at each other until Kuch finally said, "Jesus fuck, did you see those guys!"

The three of us talked about it while the sun came up.

It was good to talk, because then we didn't have to think too much about it. We figured the passenger was dead from the crash for sure, and we hoped the driver had been killed then, too, or at least knocked out. It sure looked like he'd been trying to get out that window, though.

When we got to Wenatchee we heard on the radio that it had been a couple Air Force guys on their way back to Fairchild after visiting their girl friends in Cheney. The radio said the passenger was killed instantly, but that the driver had burned to death.

Kuch and Otto both wrestled fairly well and won. If my guy hadn't been muscle-bound and overconfident about me being just a sophomore, he probably would have beat me. I didn't wrestle well at all. I had a real hard time shaking the whole scene from my mind, especially the head lolling back as if to scream. To this day I can see it. On the way home we felt the bus dip when we drove over the site of the wreck. The fire had melted the asphalt and left a low place the county hasn't filled to this day.

Otto prods me out of a light snooze. Mike Konigi stands resplendent before us.

"Huh?" asks Mike. "Huh, huh, huh, you guys? Am I spiff city or not?"

"Eat a pound, Konigi," Otto responds. Otto, like me, is clothed in the customary denim and flannel.

Konigi does look okay. He's wearing a blue double-knit blazer over a white turtleneck and gray bell-bottoms. He's wearing a white belt. I'll kill him if he's wearing white shoes. I look down at his feet. Mike Konigi lives to wrestle in Montana.

"You guys cultivate slobbery," Mike says.

"Munch a bunch, Konigi," I reply. "We're headed for a wrestling match, not the fucking Wayne Newton show at Tahoe."

"Would this stuff be okay to wear to the New Year's dance?" Mike asks seriously.

"It'd be swell," Otto says.

"Yah, it's neat," I concur.

"What's Carla going to wear?" Mike asks.

"She's got this long white dress," I reply. "It's a little more casual than a prom dress. In fact, I think it's a nightgown. It's got little yellow ducks on it. How about Keiko?"

"A long dress, too," Mike replies. "Who you gonna take, Otto?"

"I don't even know if I'll go, Mike," Otto says.

I have a great urge to chime in with some information, but I hold off for propriety's sake and because Otto would beat me up. Otto's got a giant throbbing blue-veiner for Romaine Lewis's little sister, Rayette. She is probably the most beautiful girl in town, and that includes Belle. Our critical view may be slightly clouded because Rayette is black and seems mysterious to us. But if she's not at least as beautiful as Belle, I'll eat her panties off. But then I'd like to do that, anyway.

Rayette is one of those black girls like Leeland Wain's wife, Joretta. Very delicately featured. A little turned-up nose, gigantic brown eyes, long thin bones, and tits like women in Marvel comics. The problem is she's only fifteen. Otto takes her out sometimes, I know, because Romaine told me how nice Rayette said he was.

Except for their both being tall, Romaine and Rayette look so different it's hard to believe they're brother and sister. Everyplace Rayette is delicate, Romaine is obtuse. Rayette, for example, has very thin lips. But Romaine has a nose almost exactly like a gorilla's, and as Balldozer noted Tuesday before the match, he's got lips "like the brim of a chamber pot."

"Hey!" Mike says to Otto and me. "Why don't we get a few people together and have supper at my place after the dance?"

"Great idea," I say, "but what'll I eat? I can see your mom trying to feed me all that good Japanese food. 'Sorry, Mrs. Konigi. Just a bowl of spinach, please. A little on the rare side. And a can of Nutrament for dessert.' Sure," I continue seriously. "I think Carla and I could go for that." I'll have to check to see if Carla was thinking of anything special for after the dance.

"Sounds great, Konig," says Otto. "I'll letcha know."

Mike struts back down the aisle and I turn back to the Lolo National Forest of eastern Montana.

About two seconds later Mike's little brother, Jerry, pops up besides us in an identical outfit. Jerry's, however, is all wrinkled and covered with RyKrisp crumbs. "Was Mike telling you guys how he's gonna give Keiko the big one after the dance?" Jerry asks.

"Didn't say a word about it to us, Jer," I reply.

"Don't see how he could give her the big one," Otto turns and says. "I never promised to lend him my dick."

Jerry laughs and scurries back down the aisle. We hear him laughing and repeating Otto's line until Mike bops him with a sleeping bag. We stay with families from the other schools, so we have to bring sleeping bags.

We cross the Bitterroot River, which means it's about time to get dressed. Coach is knotting his tie.

We have a rule that says David Thompson athletes have to dress presentably on road trips. That used to mean a tie and a sport coat. But last year we got it changed to include turtlenecks and letter sweaters. Still, we can't wear jeans. Otto's got a clip-on tie and a gold shirt he got for a dollar at the Safeway store. He's got the shirt on now. He scoots by me and steps into the aisle to put on his good pants. He'll wear his letter sweater, too. It's a green cardigan with a gold DT. People always give us shit about our DTs. When we walk into a match some creepo always yells out, "Oh, here come the DTs!" Then he pretends to be drunk and wobbles around yelling about seeing snakes and spiders.

In my bag I've got a gray cotton turtleneck Mom bought me for road trips when we got the rule changed and an old-fashioned sleeveless pullover letter sweater and a big floppy thug hat Carla got me for my birthday. With my baggy bell-bottomed cords I look like an escapee from *The Little Rascals* show. Mom and I used to watch them on TV together. She'd get up early for work so she'd have plenty of time to put on her makeup. I'd sit with her and we'd watch *The Little Rascals* in her room. She loved it because she used to go to their movies when she was a kid. She said they were called *Our Gang Comedy* then. I was always late for school.

I suppose it would be smarter for us to just wear our good stuff right from home instead of getting dressed on the bus. But real comfort, like old jeans and flannel shirts, is something you don't like to be without unless you absolutely have to. Not even for a six-hour bus ride.

We pull into the Custer parking lot and a few Custer and Battleground guys pelt the bus with snowballs in a friendly way. The Lewis and Clark bus isn't here yet. The door opens and the sharp cold air rushes in. On a hill behind the school, snowmobiles swarm. Either the ring of their two-cycle engines or the shot of cold air arouses Kuch from the nap he began around Coeur d'Alene. I sit and wait for him while he knots his tie and pulls his hair back into a ponytail and fixes it with a rubber band. If he can sleep through a road trip he has truly achieved tranquillity.

Schmoozler is off in a corner of the bleachers reading *Semi-Tough* to some Custer guys. They're all chortling and guffawing. We beat them in a real close match this afternoon. I felt good all through my match. It went into the third round. We stuffed my nose before I went out and it only bled a little. I got really dizzy after it was over, though. When the ref raised my arm I had to grab on to him to keep from falling down. I lay behind the bench and didn't get up until Otto went out to wrestle. Still, the gym seemed to spin when I stood up. We were down 24–20 going into Otto's match. If he hadn't pinned his man we'd have lost. The pressure was really on, but pressure doesn't bother Otto. He'd led us out for our exercises yelling, "Corega! Coreeega!" He's been fascinated with the word ever since he discovered I use that stuff instead of regular toothpaste. Coach made him captain for both the Custer and Battleground matches. Both teams have big tough heavyweights. The worst is over for us now, though. Custer is the tougher of the two, so tomorrow night should be easier.

Coach is going to have Doug Bowden wrestle in my place tomorrow night. That will give Doug some tournament experience and it will give me a little rest. Coach and I talked about it and decided missing one match wouldn't make me lose my edge. Shute is only four days away.

Otto's down behind the Lewis and Clark bench talking to Romaine. They've just finished their exercises and Battleground is out on the mat. The gym's been full all day. Most people come and go, but the really interested ones bring something to eat so they can see all the matches. I met the folks I'll be staying with. Their kid, Chris Carpenter, drew with Schmooz in a tremendous match this afternoon. Otto stops to say hello to Romaine's folks on his way back up to where we're sitting. They go to all Romaine's matches, even road trips. Rayette smiles up at Otto and I'll bet half the gym bristles with hard-ons.

I'm curled up in my sleeping bag in the Carpenter's basement under the pool table. Rance Prokoff from L.C. is asleep on the davenport. He lost pretty bad to a state champ from Battleground tonight. We shot a game of eight-ball to see who got the davenport and Rance won. Actually, it's pretty cozy under here. I've got a little desk lamp hooked up and I'm reading a book Cindy got me for Christmas. It's called *Another Roadside Attraction* and it's by a guy named Tom Robbins who lives over around Seattle. It's funny and sexy, but the thing that blows me away the furthest about it is how it fits into the stuff I'm talking about in my senior thesis. I don't know if I'm becoming monomaniacal or what, but everywhere I look I keep seeing things that fit. Robbins's characters don't believe the purpose of life is to die and be resurrected in a Christian heaven, so they aren't terribly surprised when one of them finds the mummified body of Christ where it's been stashed in the Vatican basement all these years. For a lot of people that knowledge would knock all the meaning or purpose out of living. But these Robbins people create their own meaning in the way they live. They live as though certain things were important, so those things become important. Right here Amanda says, "If our style is masterful, if it is fluid and at the same time complete, then we can recreate ourselves." A resurrection a day if you work at it. That's something I can believe in.

It's the same thing Castaneda means when he says that by the power of our will we can stop the world and remake it. And the same thing Fitzgerald shows in *The Great Gatsby* with the schedule Gatsby followed as a kid —exercising and studying needed inventions and practicing elocution and poise and reading an improving book each week and taking a bath every day. The problem with old Gatsby, though, was that he just wasn't tough enough. With all his discipline, he wasn't willing to face alone the world he'd made. He wanted Daisy along, and there was no way that stain would do anything that took independence.

I guess a lot of people are concerned about how to take charge of their lives and make them better. And not just writers, either. My own dad is trying to change. I can see him doing it. And Kuch. Kuch has put it all into his vision quest.

I think a lot about this stuff when I can't sleep. It's lonely without Carla beside me and Dad upstairs. I'm just not real comfortable in somebody else's house.

I wake to the crash of pool balls overhead. Rance is up and at it already.

"Prokoff," I growl. "If you want to live to lose a wrestling match this afternoon, you'll lighten up on that pool stick."

CRASH! Rance drills one into the corner pocket above my head. "Stay down there, Swain, or I'll clout ya on the nose." The news is really out on my tragic flaw.

"What time is it?"

"It's nine-thirty and Mrs. Carpenter says breakfast in ten minutes."

"Suppose they've got any spinach?" I ask on my way to the bathroom.

When I come out Chris Carpenter is shooting a game

with Rance. Chris looks sharp in his cowboy clothes. His eye is all puffy. "Looks like Schmoozler got a piece of your eye yesterday," I greet him.

"It's an infection," Chris replies. "I get it every season. The doctor says it's like athlete's foot."

"Typical cowboy disease," I say, smiling. "Athlete's foot of the eye." Rance laughs and Carpenter brings his stick back extra far and jabs him a firm one in the gonies. Rance shrieks in surprise and doubles over, more in reflex than in pain. Wrestlers are a playful bunch.

"Breakfast, you boys!" yells Chris's mom from upstairs.

Chris and Rance are both a couple pounds light, so they're looking forward to something substantial for breakfast. I weighed 147 on the nose after my morning dump. But since I won't wrestle tonight, I can't count on that weight loss, so I'd better go easy.

Mrs. Carpenter brings the small, thin broiled steaks on a platter. The smell elicits a growl of yearning from my stomach. I smile over my Nutrament.

Mr. and Mrs. Carpenter and Chris's younger brother and sister have a leisurely go at their pancakes and eggs. Chris's little brother, Craig, wrestled at 103 yesterday for the Custer JVs.

"Look like you'll be able to hold that weight, Louden?" Mr. Carpenter asks.

"Looks like it, sir," I reply. My stomach growls again. "May not sound like it, though," I add. We all laugh.

"We read that article about you and Gary Shute in *Sports Illustrated,*" Mrs. Carpenter says. It wasn't really an "article." It was just a couple lines and pictures of Shute and me in that "Faces in the Crowd" section they have.

"Half our team's driving over to Spokane to see you guys wrestle," Chris says.

"You better get there early," says Rance through a mouthful of steak.

We change the subject to snowmobiles. The Carpenters have two on a trailer at the side of the house. Some family strife erupts when Chris's sister, Andie, says she'd rather go snowmobiling than see Chris wrestle. Argument on the subject is short. The Carpenters are a wrestling family.

I don't feel uncomfortable this morning. It feels good to be here in the Carpenters' house. They make you feel at home.

I feel the same way about the Baldosiers, although they're a very different kind of people. They invited me for dinner about a month before they left for Brazil. Jean-Pierre and I got to know each other in physics class last year. He's the best-educated kid I know. His dad is an engineer who designs nuclear power plants. Jean-Pierre was born in France, went to grade school in Brazil, junior high in Pasco, Washington, where he got into wrestling while his dad was doing something at the Hanford Atomic Works, then high school in Spokane because his dad got a teaching job at Gonzagua U. The family left this fall to go back to Brazil so Mr. Baldosier could work on a nuclear power plant somewhere down there. Jean-Pierre is staying with the Raskas so he can finish up at David Thompson. Then he's going to college in France, where his real mother lives. That's why he isn't doing his senior thesis, the lucky bastard. He says a French college won't care whether he graduates with honors from an American high school. In fact, I think he has to take one whole year of prep courses before he can even start college there.

It was a cultural experience to have dinner with the Baldosiers. They eat like Brazilians and speak French and English and Portuguese all at once. I never get to hear many foreign languages, so it was a treat for me. I learned to say "beans" and "rice" in Portuguese and "please" and "thank you" in French. I've studied German for the past three years and never once met a person who spoke it. And that includes my German teacher. I also learned how to use my knife to push food onto my fork.

Jean-Pierre's stepmother is dark and beautiful and gracious as I imagine wives of ambassadors are gracious. She also has a maid, which probably makes being gracious a little easier. His stepsister was born in Brazil. She'd give both Belle and Rayette a run in terms of beauty, but in terms of composure and grace she seemed a world away from girls I know. Even Carla. Jean-Pierre's little brother was born in Pasco, but you'd never know it. He wears a Brazilian World Cup Soccer uniform all the time and won't speak anything but Portuguese.

We all talked about politics and atomic energy and "futebol," which is what Carlos Henrique, the little brother, calls soccer. And the neat thing was that everybody got to talk and everybody got listened to. Mr. and Mrs. Baldosier and Jean-Pierre stopped and waited to hear Lucia out on her condemnation of torture in Brazil and they deferred to Carlos Henrique on the sad state of French futebol. Lucia shared some false information about heavy water and Jean-Pierre set her straight patiently. Then his dad set him straighter, and just as patiently. I guess I'd just never seen a family pay that much attention to each other. But then, most of the families I know don't even take the time to sit down together. Sometimes I sure wish I had some brothers and sisters.

We're headed out of Missoula after munching up a whole bunch of Battleground Bluecoats. Doug Bowden stole the show at fifty-four by beating Battleground's undefeated Ray Rilke, whom I am glad I didn't have to wrestle. It was an especially big victory for Doug and the whole team because if Doug can beat guys like Rilke, losing me isn't going to make any difference.

When Otto found out Doug was wrestling in my place he went to Coach and asked if Doug could be captain. Coach thanked Otto and said sure. Coach would never have said a thing if Otto hadn't suggested it.

Doug went right after Rilke, which is something Rilke wasn't used to. Most guys, if they think you're tough, will hang back and wrestle defensively. As a team we reject that philosophy, but we do have a couple guys who occasionally experience failures of faith. But that's okay, because wrestling isn't really a team sport. It could be that Rilke is so fucking strong and tough-looking nobody has tried to push him around before, because when Doug took it to him at the whistle, Rilke acted like he'd wandered into the girls' bathroom. Balldozer says Rilke "wants to fart higher than his hole," which I guess means he's arrogant. After Doug took him down, Rilke regained his composure and reversed him in a flash. Doug didn't seem real impressed, however, because he boomed right to his feet and rolled Rilke to his back. Unfortunately, he rolled him off the mat. There were some heavy sighs in the Battleground bleachers at that move.

Doug wrestled that match in one explosion of energy right after another, which is what it takes against tough guys. With about half a minute left in the match he spun into a short sitout. Rilke freaked and tried to drive Doug's head down between his legs. I guess he was just trying to keep Doug from switching him. But he drove into Doug way too hard and Doug just let Rilke push him to his feet. Then Doug rolled him the exact same way he had in the first round. Except this time he rolled him in bounds.

Time ran out before Doug could pin him, but he got the near-fall points and won the match. The bench just went fucking insane. Coach was leaping up and down and shouting. He had let me sit beside him with the team. Kuch, who lay behind the bench in semi-exhaustion after his very tough win, whooped and yipped and banged his hands and feet on the floor. We mobbed the mat to get Doug, and in the confusion Coach Morgan conked me in the nose with his tape recorder. He slung it over his shoulder, probably to be sure not to lose it, and BLAM —I got his TEAC smack on my nose. I can't even watch a wrestling match without getting my nose bloodied. I soaked my letter sweater in cold water right after I congratulated Doug.

I returned from the bathroom in time to see Balldozer wrestle what I consider to be the best match of his career at David Thompson. Even though he did get beat 6–3. He lost to Dan Klosterman, a two-time state champ and one of the best wrestlers in the Northwest and maybe the whole country. Balldozer is good—strong and fast and loaded with guts—but his balance just isn't what it could be. And if you haven't got that, you just can't beat the good guys. He did everything right and looked beautiful.

Balldozer is this sort of Greco-Roman–looking, incredibly handsome guy. Shute is handsome that way. Shute and Balldozer look a lot alike, in fact. Balldozer is the giant economy size, though. I think if I weren't a pretty fair wrestler and a semigood student, I'd feel inferior around Balldozer just because he's so good-looking. I've got to get over that. I plan to tell him what a good match he wrestled, but the bastard's drinking a peanut butter milkshake, and I'm afraid if I get near enough to smell it, I'll roll him for it.

We stopped for burgers at Denny's on the way out of town. I drank a tea. I figured I'd lost that much weight just watching the match. Boy, it's weird to just sit and watch. I kept thinking what I'd do if I were out there. It was frustrating. I'll watch the guys wrestle out their season and I'll go to the district and state tournaments, but it's sure going to feel weird just watching.

Shute and his dad were sitting at the counter when we trooped in. Poor fuckers. They drove all the way over here to watch me wrestle Rilke. I wonder why they did it. I'm sure they've got just as much film of me as we do of Gary.

Gary and his dad look like brothers. Like brother plumb bobs. I wonder if you can make hair go straight back and wavy like theirs, or if you have to be born that way. Mr. Shute isn't real young, I don't think, but he's in great shape, and whenever I see him he's always in jeans and a tanker jacket, which is a pretty youthful outfit. He's a plumber, so he gets lots of exercise. They also hunt and fish a lot.

I'd talked to Gary for a minute at the match, but I wanted just to say hello again, so I stopped.

"Hi, Gary," I said. "Hi, Mr. Shute." I shook hands with his dad.

"I don't know what you guys are gonna do without anybody at fifty-four," Mr. Shute said and winked. Everybody in the gym was blown away by how good Doug was.

I sat down next to Gary.

"Have you seen this?" His dad handed the *Sports Illustrated* clipping across to me.

"We're famous." I smiled and punched Gary a light one in the ribs. I've sure taken better pictures than that. Gary looks like Frank Gifford from *Monday Night Football* and I look like old Harpo Marx from *A Night at the Opera*. The bastard photographer caught me right after practice. My hair was all standing up and someone had just made me laugh. I look like I was being electrocuted.

Mr. Shute folded it up and put it back in his wallet. He finished his coffee and Gary finished his Jell-O. Gary said he'd look for me at the New Year's dance and they left after we shook hands. Gary stopped a second to congratulate Doug and Jean-Pierre on their good matches. His dad said hello to Coach and they were out the door and off in their pickup.

It's nearly two o'clock. All the inside lights are off, so out the window you can see the snow blowing down and swirling from the trees. Good cheer lasted almost to the Idaho line. Kuch loves beating Custer and Battleground. After both matches he walked into their locker rooms and invited them all to come to Spokane and visit him on the twenty-fifth of June so together they could celebrate the great victory at the Greasy Grass. "What the fuck is that?" a couple guys asked. "Custer's last stand," Kuch smiled. The Custer and Battleground guys got a kick out of it, but the Custer coach asked us to leave.

Just after we pulled out of Denny's parking lot, Otto called out above the din, "Hey, Coach! How about next year you don't get us up so early just to go beat up a bunch of cowboys and miners!"

"Yah, yah, yah!" everybody yelled. Before Coach could respond, Schmoozler declared in a firm cadence, "We're not gonna be here next year, Turd Head." The bus went a little quieter for a minute or two while the seniors thought that one over. But the noise picked right back up. Coach promised never again to get Otto out of bed to beat up a cowboy or a miner.

I talked to Balldozer awhile. He also thinks tonight's match was his best ever. We listened to Schmoozler's tape for a while. I snatched it when Schmooz fell asleep. Balldozer's asleep now, too. The bus driver and I are probably the only ones awake. Sausage and Little Konigi may be awake back there somewhere, though, still trying to determine which girls in the sophomore class are ripe for the large one.

It's amazing. Balldozer's grandparents in France live in a house that's been in their family since right before the French Revolution. That's 183 years. He says the house is even older than that. The stones have scars from two world wars. He says they have a room with paintings of all the Baldosiers up until the invention of the camera and then they have photographs. It must be neat to know where you come from. The relatives on his mom's side are Spanish, which must account for Jean-Pierre's darkness.

He wasn't terribly impressed with my thesis as I summarized it. I guess he's more classical in his approach to things. Like when we talk about the meaning and importance of different things in life, I bring up Fitzgerald and Agee and Carlos Castaneda and other fairly contemporary guys like that. But Balldozer always talks about Rousseau and Voltaire and Montaigne and Shakespeare and other guys long dead. Once he brought up Chief Joseph, but that was probably because he'd just come back from a camping trip with Kuch.

I explained about the myth of self-discovery—that this stuff about a person "finding himself" and having the world then fall into place around him is wishful bullshit, and that what really happens among the few people who make it happen is not that they find themselves but that they "define" themselves. I used the example of Bob Dylan from the Scaduto biography Kuch gave me for my birthday. Dylan wanted to be a folk-hero–singer, so he made up a history, went on the road and followed the tradition, worked hard, and by the power of his will and imagination became his dream and probably more.

I talked about how, even if you define yourself as a

Christian and believe in eternal life, you've got to realize your time on earth is incredibly short. And I explained further that along with this has to go the realization that we not only die alone, but that, really, we live alone, too. That no matter how we love our families and friends, we can't breathe for each other when our alveoli clog up with cigarette smoke and car exhaust, that we can't pee for each other when our kidneys stop working, and that we can't really comfort each other once we know these things. This is the real reason Thomas Wolfe couldn't go home again and why old Don Genaro won't ever reach Ixtlan and most of all why we've got to love the people who deserve it as fiercely as we love our own lives.

And then Balldozer says, "Oh, you're writing about growing up." I passed over the remark and went on. But now the bastard's got me wondering.

S unday night is sure a weird night for a dance. But it's New Year's Eve and that's when the dance is traditionally held. I feel as though I should be doing leftover homework. I think I'd like to see Christmas and New Year's made Wednesday every year. Carla notes, however, that there's a sense of orderliness in beginning a new week and a new year on the same day.

Although she denies responsibility, I'm blaming Carla for some embarrassment I suffered this afternoon. Actually, it was the fault of general fatigue and my often intractable libido, but it's more fun to blame Carla.

I was really, really tired last night. I puzzled over Balldozer's comment until I fell asleep. I vaguely remember him waking me in the school parking lot and Carla driving me home. I remember flopping into bed and Katzenburger licking my face, or maybe it was Carla taking advantage of me. Anyway, I was dog tired.

I got up around nine and ran three miles and came home and did a workout in the laundry room. I started my laundry-room workouts again because without school and work I was afraid I wouldn't burn enough energy to keep my weight down. I start the school year with my laundry-room workouts and only give them up when I feel really in good shape. I take my tape player in and put on a special workout tape. I keep the tape player in a plastic bag so the moisture doesn't get to it. I dry a load of laundry so the room's good and hot and I wear my rubber sweat suit under my cotton one. I've got ten songs on my tape. I skip rope through one song, stop the tape, do a hundred pushups, then a hundred sits, then turn the next song on and do it till the tape is over. Sometimes, between the music and the exercise and the heat, I really get spacy. I start out skipping to "Dancing in the Moonlight," which always makes me think of drinking beer on summer evenings down under the Hangman Creek bridge. Then I go through "Family Affair," "Treat Her like a Lady," "Respect Yourself," and five other good ones, so that by the time I get to the long version of "Layla" I believe myself to be the toughest, meanest, most inshapest, baddest-ass kid on the block. I'm also near death.

Anyway, I finished my laundry-room workout and took off my soggy clothes and was headed for the shower when I saw Carla reading in front of the fireplace and decided to bedevil her some. I tiptoed up behind her and lay my wasted cock gently on her shoulder. She didn't respond for a few seconds; then she turned her head a little and glanced down at the thing. "What's that look like?" I asked.

She studied it a bit. Finally she responded. "Well," she said. "It looks like a cock, I guess . . . only smaller."

I hadn't expected it was quite that wasted. I began to whimper and crept over to the davenport and curled up in a fetal position. Carla cast aside her book and kitten and hurried over to me. After a minute or two she sat up and faced me. "It's beginning to look more like a cock all the time," she said very sweetly.

We hadn't made love for two and a half days. We slid along the linoleum like brazen bobsledders. We did the monkey in the banana tree, the grasshopper and the leaf, we practiced our tandem bearwalk. We ended up on the bed.

I tried to sit up afterward, but one workout on top of another was just too much. I rose to a sitting position but couldn't hold it and fell backward the other ninety degrees. Before my eyes Carla's rusty muff glistened postcoitally. We fell asleep, each pillowed on the other's thigh.

I awoke in a spasm of guilt. Coach had scheduled a practice just for my benefit at 3:30. It was 3:25, so I didn't have time to shower. I jumped into my clammy sweat suits, laced up my boots, and made a run for it.

I burst through the locker-room door in a sweat. Coach was the only one still downstairs. "Sorry, Coach," I said. "Went running without my watch."

"It's okay," he said. He smiled big and patted me on the shoulder. I grabbed my wrestling shoes and followed him upstairs. Coach turned into the film room to set up the films on Shute for tomorrow.

In the wrestling room Kuch and Doug and Smith and Balldozer and Otto lay around the mats in various attitudes of repose. I flopped down on my back and began to bridge up on my neck to get loose. Right away Kuch began to sniff loudly. He sniffed and sniffed. He crawled over next to me and sniffed along my back and down my arm all the way to the ends of my fingers. He called the guys over for a consultation. Full of curiosity they tumbled across the mats. I quit bridging and just sat down and rested my chin in my palm.

"It's possum," Kuch said.

Otto poked his head close and sniffed loudly. "Good thing Sausage and Little Konigi aren't here, Swain. They'd chew your mustache off."

Bowden sniffed long and looked at Kuch. "Is that really what it smells like?" he asked.

"That's the scent, all right," Kuch replied. "But usually you'll find it more attractively wrapped."

"It appears you've been playing the drooling clarinet," observed Balldozer.

"You guys ate nothin' but spinach all the time, you'd smell funny, too," I declared.

They made me take a shower before they'd start the workout. They told Coach I just ran downstairs for some nose stoppers. Only he had been gentleman enough to ignore it.

The dance is at the Spokane Club, which is a pretty spiffy place. We've risen to it, though, at least in terms of apparel. Carla's in her long soft white dress with the little ducks and I'm in my white denim suit. It's fun to dress up sometimes.

Mom wanted me to have a suit so I'd look decent when I visited the University of Oklahoma last spring. She said I could charge it on her account at the Bon Marché. It's pretty racy. The pants are pleated and flared wide and it's got a white vest with pockets I stick my fingers in and look dignified. Mom wished she'd gone with me to pick it out. She said I looked like a pimp.

It's snowing like crazy. It started as I was running home from practice. We've got about six new inches already. Carla looks ethereal in her mad dash to the door. She says none of her coats go with her long dress, so she's not wearing one. In the white dress she seems to float through the falling snow. Her hair is rich and warm and it shines in the light. I sit watching her until she's inside. She turns and waves. I wave back, thinking just in a flash how beautiful she is and how lucky I am. Some impatient creepo jolts me out of my brief reverie with a couple strong blasts on his horn. I churn politely off in the DeSoto. My great blue boat, my grand hotel, my time machine.

I couldn't find a parking place closer than two blocks, so my suit droops a little by the time I reach the door. Right away Carla sends me to the men's room to towel off. My hair is lightly frosted with snow. I don't have a nice coat either, but at least I should have thought to bring an umbrella. In a little while I'll work up a good dancin' sweat and nobody'll know the difference.

Off in a corner we spot Schmooz and Karen and Kuch and Laurie. Schmooz is president of the social club that's cosponsoring the dance. Besides wrestling and selling clothes part-time at the Klothes Kloset, he makes time for the club. He invited a lot of the guys on the team to join, but most of us just have other priorities, I guess. Also, Schmooz is about the only guy in the club I feel like I have much in common with. They're not bad guys or anything, although I can't say I'm crazy about their initiation rites. Belle is in the girls' club that's the other cosponsor. She was after Carla to join for a while, but Carla finally convinced her she'd had her fill of that sort of thing in Chicago. I think the girls' club is a little more exclusive than the guys'. I belong to the Lettermen's club at school. I'm not against clubs or anything. Dad kind of is now, though. He dropped out of the Moose Lodge because they wouldn't let me in their gym when my hair was long and geodesic.

We say hello all around. Carla grabs Schmooz and gives him a vigorous head rub. Schmooz is short and broad. He swoons against Carla's bra-less breast. Because of the double lures of his curly blond mane and the animal onomatopoeia of his name, Carla is unable to keep from fondling him.

Toward us walk Romaine and a girl I don't know and Otto and Rayette. Otto and Rayette look like they come from heaven they're so beautiful. In his rented blue suit Otto looks like the world's biggest, toughest stockbroker. Rayette looks like an African angel in her long, sky-blue robes. Her eyes are huge and brown and remind me of deer's eyes. Otto is self-conscious because she's so young, but I guess he couldn't resist.

Mike and Keiko arrive and head in our direction. Behind them Belle and Tanneran stand in the doorway. They spot us and wave. "Hi, folksies!" Belle shouts. Tanneran is a chaperone. They walk upstairs to join Leeland and Joretta Wain, who are chaperones, too. They all sit at a table on the balcony that surrounds the dance floor.

I've been very nervous lately, thinking of the match, but I feel it slipping away now. It's fun to dance and laugh and forget it all for a while, even though I know I'll wake up to it again in the morning.

The first band is called "Soul Food." They're a bunch of older guys, mostly black, who used to be the house band at Rollie's Ribs. They get into "I Heard It through the Grapevine" and lure Leeland and Joretta down from the balcony. Carla and I just stand awhile and watch them dance.

One night when Carla and I were babysitting their little girls, Leeland and Joretta came home really high from dancing somewhere and put on some of their old records and taught us to do the Boogaloo, which is a dance they said they used to do in college. They're doing it now. So are Romaine and Rayette as Otto and Romaine's date look on. It looks an awful lot like a mating ritual. They move and turn and do everything together, but they don't touch. It's no cliché or ethnic slur to say black people have great rhythm. I'd call it one of the eternal verities.

We sit on the balcony while the bands change. Everybody is psyched to see Sausage play. He really is something of a prodigy. The band he plays with is all college guys except for him. They travel all over the Northwest and make some pretty heavy bread. Sausage wants to go on the road with them when the season's over, but his folks won't let him. Not even just weekends.

I notice Belle is hanging on to Tanneran for dear life. She looks about half in love.

Otto is demonstrating to Leeland and Joretta how to dance like a New Guinea mud person. He assumes the attitude of a spear-wielding orangutan and grunts a lot and thumps around in a circle. Everybody laughs. I notice Rayette's big brown eyes seem only for Otto, which makes me happy. Otto says if he can't play pro ball he wants to be a bartender or go to New Guinea and be a mud person.

Sausage is just blowing his head off on the flute. He's weaving in the flashing lights and blowing sweet bird sounds. His band seems to be influenced by Chicago and Santana, with Sausage adding a flavor of Jethro Tull. They're kind of hard to dance to, but people are dancing anyway. Carla and I just stand close and watch. She leans back against me. I hold her lightly around the waist. She bangs her head against my chest softly, like a baby will. Sausage turns our way and we take a few steps back. Against the red and blue lights tiny sparks of spittle fly.

The band takes its break ten minutes before midnight. The lights come up and Sausage comes down and says hello. We tell him how great he's doing. He's all smiles and sweat. Shute and his girl friend come over. It's interesting that she's not especially good-looking and a little taller than he is. We introduce all around. They both tell Sausage how much they like the music. Gary looks at his watch and sees it's almost midnight. We wish each other a Happy New Year.

The noise level rises inside, and from outside horns honk and a few firecrackers explode. It's 1973. I shake hands with Sausage and wish him a Happy New Year. Carla kisses him a friendly one on the lips. The Sausage Man blushes. "My first groupie of the new year," he says, beaming. He asks us when we're leaving for Konigi's and I tell him 12:30. He's got to stay till two.

Otto and Rayette come over to say Happy New Year. I give Rayette a little peck. She's slightly surprised, but quickly regains her composure. I've never kissed a black girl before. It's fun, but no different.

Kuch and Laurie come over. We wave up to Leeland and Joretta and Gene and Belle on the balcony. "Happy New Year, folksies!" Belle yells down.

We dance slowly into the new year, holding tight. The band plays Santana's "Samba Pa Ti." We just float around in the beautiful music. Carla's hair smells like herb tea.

Sausage and the lead guitar player take turns with the melody. They both play it so clean and sharp. It's funny to see Sausage do something with so much poise. You'd never guess that most of the time he's just a dumb kid like the rest of us. It makes me proud of him. We clap a lot when the song is over and wave Sausage good night.

The Konigi house looks like a shopping center with all their Christmas lights and all the cars. Mrs. Konigi greets us at the door. Many dark shapes stand around the long dining room table. They seem to stare obliquely at the assortment of good eats. I guess we're last to arrive.

183

Sushi, teriyaki, rice balls wrapped in seaweed, almond chicken, and other as yet unnamed yummies quaver in the soft candlelight. Behind us Mrs. Konigi switches on the lights revealing Coach, the David Thompson varsity wrestling team, and assorted girl friends. Some people laugh, some cheer. Mike Konigi leads me to the head of the table. He seats me before a plate heaped with steaming spinach. A small gold flag protrudes from the green glob like a buttercup from a cow pie. On the gold flag is written in green: "Good luck, Louden!"

I think Carla's finally finished throwing up. She had an allergic reaction to the ginger in the teriyaki. She knew she was allergic to ginger, but she didn't know they put it in teriyaki sauce. She stays kneeling at the toilet while I get a glass of cold water and a wash cloth for her face. She's weak and shaky and her nightie sticks to her sweaty back. Throwing up is hard work. Katzenburger peeks out of the wastepaper basket. "Poor Katzen," Carla gasps. "I scared the Katzen."

She feels a lot better and falls asleep almost the second her head hits the pillow. Katzen sits on my chest. She idles smoothly and her tiny eyes catch the slip of light from under the door and reflect it in a green-gold glow.

Dad was worried and wanted to take Carla to the hospital but between barfs she talked him out of it. He's back in bed now. Cindy and Willa were here. Dad said they watched TV and babysat Willa while she babysat the cat. I didn't realize Dad was such a sucker for little kids. I thought guys his age were over that. He gives Willa roller-coaster rides on his knee and horsey rides on his back. He buys her animal books with lots of pictures and reads them to her on his lap.

A couple months ago when I was in the very most agonizing stages of my diet, Carla ran upstairs one morning and fainted in the kitchen. Dad and I had just the day before commented that she seemed to be losing weight. As she sat in a kitchen chair getting some of her color back, Dad began to ask her questions.

"Carla." He bent to look her in the face. "Have you been losing weight?"

"A couple pounds," Carla replied.

"Have you been feeling sick in the mornings?"

Carla and I looked at each other. Dad thought she was pregnant.

"I've been dieting," Carla explained in a reassuring voice. "I can't stand to eat while Louden starves himself."

That was a surprise to both Dad and me. I told Carla please to eat and assured her that in a couple months I'd be eating like my old pig self again.

Dad wanted to pursue it. "Look," he said to both of us. "You two have a home under my roof as long as you want and you can live here any way you want. But you've got to be careful about your futures. Don't let things get out of control."

He looked like he was going on, but Carla interrupted. "Dad," she said, "I'm not pregnant and I'm not going to get pregnant."

"Well, you've got to be sure to use—"

"Condoms," I interrupted. Carla had been taking pills but I'd convinced her to stop.

"Rubbers." Carla smiled.

"Prophylactics." Dad nodded.

"Worth a pound of cure." I smiled at Carla.

"I'm hungry," she said.

I've just realized a funny thing. This is the first New Year's Eve in my life I haven't either been with Mom and

Dad at midnight or talked to them on the phone to wish them a Happy New Year. My first impulse is to run upstairs right now to tell Dad Happy New Year and call Mom. By God, I'm going to.

Katzen squeaks as I lift her off my chest and tuck her under the covers. Carla is dead to the world. Dad's door is closed and I don't hear the TV. He must be asleep. It's nearly two o'clock. I guess I can tell him in the morning. I should probably wait till then to call Mom, too.

XXII

I t's still snowing as I run back from practice. I can't believe it. It started on my way running home from practice yesterday, so that makes about twenty-four hours of straight snow. Everything is deeply covered and there's a great softness even my running bootfalls can't break. Shoveling the walk will be a perfect way to begin tomorrow. It'll loosen me up without making me real tired. I hope Dad hasn't already shoveled.

We watched a couple films of Shute and had a brief workout, in which I was absolutely unstoppable. Probably because everybody but me was still filled with Japanese food from Konigi's. I tried wrestling without anything in my nose and it didn't bleed a bit. Coach and I figured that maybe the nose stoppers have been irritating the inside of my nose and making it bleed rather than protecting it. I won't use any tomorrow.

Coach showed a film of Shute's match last week against Palouse and then another of him at last year's state tournament. Then he showed the first one again.

Kuch and Otto and I thought Shute looked better in the film from last year. But Coach said not to count on it, because Shute was probably a lot more psyched for the state tournament than for a duel meet with Palouse. That's probably true. The Palouse film didn't show much, anyway. Shute pinned his man in the first round. "That guy is faster than a fart on an oilskin," Balldozer said. I think the French have an inordinate concern with flatulence. Bowden and Smith couldn't come today because their families went out of town for New Year's dinner. I made sure to thank Coach and the guys again for last night and for coming on New Year's to watch films and help me work out.

Shute looks real, real good. He may be faster than I am but I don't think he's stronger or has any better balance or knows his moves any better. He's aggressive all the time, but he doesn't seem to like to spend much time on his feet. I've noticed it before and I saw it again today in the films. I noticed in the state tournament film that he went for the takedown just as soon as he could and always tried to reverse rather than escape. Maybe I'll try to spend a lot of time on my feet with him.

I hope he wins the coin toss. If he does, it means their first wrestler gets the choice of positions in the second round. Then in the next match our guy gets to choose. It'll work out so I'll have my choice, and that's important. You always want to choose the top position in the second round so you can be on the bottom in the third and score yourself some points. All you can do from the top position is try to pin the guy, and against guys like Shute that's just not done.

I wish he weren't shorter than I am and so goddamn good-looking. Why can't he be cretinous, monosyllabic, or maybe look like the Hunchback of Notre Dame instead of an anatomy sketch by Michelangelo? It makes me feel like the bad guy.

Down the street Cindy's Mazda pulls up in front of the house. Willa leaps out into the fresh snow and disappears. Cindy hauls her out and shakes her off. Dad hasn't shoveled yet. The little kid laughs like crazy and hollers for more. I fling her into the softest-looking mounds and hoist her back out until she begins to turn blue. It doesn't take long. Then the three of us head in for New Year's dinner.

This afternoon I ate what I believe to be the last spinach of my life. I weighed 147 after an ugly green shit, so I think I can safely look forward to a can of Nutrament for breakfast. I thought I'd go see *Jesus Christ Superstar* for a little inspiration tonight, but I finally decided against it. I ran another three miles and did a laundry-room workout instead. I got off on a great fantasy about doctoring in a space settlement. One of Jupiter's moons was just like the earth around 1800 and I got to see the land before all the people came. I inoculated the Indians against all the diseases we probably brought them. Then I took a shower and Carla got naked with me and we looked at ourselves in the bathroom mirror like we used to do pretty often after we came back from our first camping trip. It's a little ritual we still do, but not as regularly as before. I identify my different muscles, then flex them one by one as best I can. It's how I studied for anatomy tests. I start with the thick cords in my neck, the sternocleidomastoids; then I hit the high spots all the way down to my gastrocnemius muscles. I don't have real big calves but they're pretty well defined. In fact, bodywise, I'm every bit as good-looking as Shute. We put on our Pachelbel record and looked at each other and poked different places and laughed a lot. It's kind of hard to spot some of Carla's muscles, so I have to feel around for them. She thinks I should be able to flex my cock. I grunt and strain, but she always has to lend a hand.

I've finished typing almost the last of my senior thesis. I only have the conclusion left. Maybe I can write it tomorrow night when the match is over and my nervousness is gone. It shouldn't be more than a couple paragraphs. I'm thinking hard about what Balldozer said about it all being nothing more than the process of growing up. Maybe that's what my conclusion should be. But if Balldozer's right, I bet damn few people ever really grow up.

I'm so nervous I couldn't even make love. I probably could have, but I sure wouldn't have been very good. I told Carla and she held me and gave me lots of kisses and told me it would all be over tomorrow and that we could make love several times then. I couldn't sit still. My stomach was roiling with nervousness, so I decided to type. I called Mom this morning to wish her a Happy New Year and found out she and her husband, Arney, are driving over to see the match. I couldn't talk her out of it. I hate to have them come all that way just to watch me wrestle. I always get nervous before a match, but this is the worst ever.

XXIII

I t's finally stopped snowing and the morning is beautiful. Before I finally hit the sack last night I taped a note to the coffee pot reminding Dad please not to shovel the walk. Sometimes he gets up early and shovels before work. I slept late. It's almost ten. Carla left a note telling me not to be nervous. I usually feel logy when I sleep so late, but I feel okay this morning. Aside from being nervous. Whenever I tell Dad I'm nervous he always tells me to have confidence. I have all the confidence in the fucking world. I'm just nervous is all.

I shovel slowly and with deliberation. The snow is so deep I can't push it as usual. I dig down to concrete, then take it shovelful by shovelful. Mr. Sears yells from across the street do I want to use his snow blower. I shout back no thanks. He waves through the white mist thrown up by his machine and yells me good luck tonight. When I finish, the snowbanks are so high the sidewalk seems like a tunnel. They're higher than my head.

It's 3:30. I'm just getting more and more nervous

hanging around home. I can't take a nap, I don't feel like reading, and there's nothing but shit on TV, so I guess I'll take a slow walk up to school. I call Dad to let him know I'm leaving early and that he won't need to call and wake me up.

"Good luck, Son. Do your best."

"Thanks, Dad. I will."

It's all we ever say. I guess it's all there is to say. But just once I wish he'd tell me, "Go out there and make 'em remember us, Louden! Bulge and snap! Crack, zing, whip, dance, and fly! Write the name of Swain in shivers up everybody's spine!" Dad would never tell me that. But maybe he's thinking it. If he were just thinking it, I'd be happy.

Leeland Wain is in the gym, shooting at one of the side baskets with his two little girls. The mats have already been taped down in the middle of the floor. Carts and carts of folding chairs jam the doorway by the ticket booth. Sharon and Rosalie see me and run across the floor in that funny way little girls run. They're twins. They wear matching maroon jogging suits and tiny white Adidas shoes. Joretta tied their hair in about a zillion little corn rows. They get up to me and I turn around and open my hands, palms up, behind my back. They each slap my hands. Then they turn around. I slap their little hands solidly and the three of us shuck and jive across the gym floor to their daddy. Leeland flips me the ball. I shoot and miss the rim by ten yards. He laughs. I rebound for them awhile. Leeland asks me what I'm doing up here so early. I tell him I'm nervous. He laughs. "Shute's the one oughta be nervous," he says.

"Louden's gonna whup 'im! Louden's gonna whup 'im!" Sharon and Rosalie yell. They do a few cheerleader motions, run around in a couple circles, then collapse in a burst of giggles. "You girls is dummies," Leeland says in his Bill Cosby voice. He bounces the basketball all around their heads as they continue to giggle and each tries to hide under the other.

"Good luck, man!" Leeland shouts after me, swishing one from the top of the key.

I walk around the halls awhile. I wind up on the fourth floor and stand looking out through the darkness at the park. Then it's five o'clock and time to weigh in.

We approach the scale in a double line of naked bodies. The ref stands behind the scale. Coach Ratta stands on our side and Charlie Swann, the Evergreen coach, stands on theirs.

The ref sets the weight at 147. Shute gets on. The ref removes his thumb and lets the balance fall. It stops in the middle. He holds it up again. I get on. The balance falls slowly to the middle and stops dead.

I can't get excited about the JV matches. I take a look out the window at the crowd and feel like throwing up. Chairs surround the mats ten rows deep and bleachers surround the chairs. Every seat and all standing room look taken.

Kuch's uniform feels weird. It's too tight. Bowden stands at the window, hollering down at Marty Ryan, who's wrestling 154 JV. Doug's name looks strange over the big 154 on the back of the warm-up top I've worn so often the past two and a half years.

Beside me Kuch squats Indian fashion in his street clothes and Otto lies with his eyes closed and his feet up on the wall as usual. Nobody says anything. I lie flat on my back on the mat. I'm so nervous I'm breathing through my mouth. I fit the little ear plug in my ear and close my eyes. I feel for the second button on my tape player and push it down. Electric wind blows in my ear for a second; then a dam bursts through my head. Mist falls and I shiver with the first few drops. I slow my breathing and fold my hands on my chest.

Coach comes up and says the JVs lost it. He tells us not to be nervous about the big crowd. What it sounds like down there is the goddamn Superbowl.

In our moment of silence I think about the millions of factors that combined to bring about this moment. I controlled a few, but most I had no control of. I made the decision to lose the weight and wrestle Shute and I trained hard. But I can't take credit for my birth as a healthy male in a relatively loving family with enough to eat. And it wasn't me who set things up so the wrestling bus arrived after the VW hit the gas truck near Cheney our sophomore year. A few minutes earlier and it could have been us. I realize my eighteen years have been full of real good luck. Silently I thank my parents for the gift of life.

We stand in the dark behind the gym doors. Through the little window all I see are the backs of people's heads. I'm sort of paralyzed. It sounds like they're going crazy in there.

"Whatcha waitin' for?" asks Otto from the darkness behind me.

"I can't think of anything to yell."

"You've gotta yell somethin'. You're the fucking captain!"

Coach pokes his head in to see what's holding us up. "What you guys doing?"

"Swain can't think of anything to yell," says Otto.

"I can't think of a thing, Coach," I confess.

"Banzai! Banzai!" yells Coach as he shoves me

through the doors and runs beside me, weaving through the people and between the bleachers and the chairs. He drops off when we hit the mats. I lead the guys around the big circle a couple times, then into our exercises. The sound of Kuch's braid slapping the mat is notably absent.

I'm watching Shute lead Evergreen through their exercises when I'm tapped on the shoulder. It's Mom and her husband. I get up and give Mom a kiss and shake hands with Arney. She looks good. I think maybe she's put on weight. But she'll melt away to nothing if she doesn't take off that dumb fur coat. I take them to the bleachers, where Mr. and Mrs. Konigi promised to save them seats. The Konigis squinch one way and the people next to them squinch the other way, creating a space. Dad spots Mom and Arney and Mom spots Dad and Cindy. For a second nothing happens. Then they both put on smiles and wave. I go back to the bench. Carla waves to Mom from her seat with Tanneran and the Wain family. Belle sits on the floor, leaning back into Gene's lap. She's wearing her Rolling Stones panties. They're gold and they've got that big red Rolling Stones tongue sewn on the crotch.

Shute and I go out for the coin toss. He looks serene. I suppose I look the same. Gary calls heads, but the ref's quarter comes up tails. I win the toss. Shit. That means our first wrestler gets his choice of top or bottom in the second round. It will work out so that Gary'll have the choice in our match. And he'll choose top so he'll be on bottom in the third round. If there is a third round. Shit. I wanted the choice. I guess I'll have to score my points in rounds one and two. The David Thompson fans scream happily as Gary and I shake hands and return to our benches.

I twist my jump rope into knots watching Little Konigi and the Sausage Man lose. Raska wins and Mike Konigi pins his man. The closer it gets to my match, the calmer I become. Even in this madhouse. That's the way it always is. Seeley gets pinned. Schmooz beats Terry Muzzy, who beat him for the district championship last year. Williamson is doing okay in the first round as I walk behind the bench to get warm. I glance over and see Gary get up, too.

It seems like the crowd cheers every step I take, every whack of my rope against the warm-up mat. Evergreen cheers Gary just as crazily.

I reverse the rope a time or two and our fans yell and stomp as though I were scoring points. Some Evergreen fans jeer and call me a hotdog.

I do a few pushups and stretch my groin. Bridging from my back to my neck, I see a Channel 4 camera guy shooting video tape of me. He shoots me while I look upside down. He's balding and he reminds me of Lemon Pie. And Lemon Pie reminds me that in about seven minutes my life will be back to normal. I'll study during the day and work at night. I'll develop a new routine and maybe make some new friends and enlarge my world a little.

Williamson lets his man escape just at the buzzer and loses by a point.

"Shit to the thirteenth, man!" shouts Balldozer as I walk out to the mats.

"Banzai, man! Banzai!" yells the Big Konig. "May you live a thousand years!"

I hear everything, as I always do.

Kuch yelps and yips and screams, "Munch 'im up, Swain! Munch 'im up!"

"It's dinner time!" yells Otto. "Eat 'im, eat 'im, eat 'im, eat 'im!" All the guys chime in.

From the bleachers Leeland and Joretta and Sharon and Rosalie wave clenched fists. Tanneran screams unintelligibly. Dad claps and Cindy chants, "WIN . . . WIN . . ." along with the cheerleaders. Mom looks worried. Arney claps along with the chant. Carla smiles and shines and doesn't make a sound.

I'm calm as I enter the circle. Behind me trails a brief tradition. It's made up, but it's mine. Win or lose, the river flows again.

Shute and I cross and shake hands. The whistle blows. Through me flows the power to blast Grand Coulee Dam to smithereens.